Even the Devil was once an Angel

The names have been changed to protect the innocent and those that are guilty as hell.

Also by Adisa Salim

True Confessions of a Real Life B.A.P.

Heavy lies the head that wears the crown

The Adventures of Loc and Platt

Dedications and Acknowledgements

This book is dedicated to my niece, Veronica Harris
For accepting and loving me as I am
Thank you for being more than family, you are a true friend
A rarity of beauty and grace
You are truly loved and appreciated

Eric Beck, thank you for going through this crazy journey with me.
Thanks for being open to the possibilities
Enlightened to the truth
And fearless in the face of adversity
You have been an amazing friend to me and I'm sorry if
I ever took our friendship for granted. I love you, Mr. Beck

Vickey MyReality Williams, thank you, my beautiful sister for
stepping up and being a friend. You are such a kind hearted and
generous person. Much love and respect, Queen.

Finally, thank you to my brother, Dwain Stanford. You are the light
that leads my path. I am fortunate to have you as not only a brother
but a friend. You are so insightful. Thank you for always sharing
your knowledge with me. I love you to the moon and back.
Thanks to all those that have supported me as both an Author and a
Spoken Word Artist. I truly appreciate each and every one of you. I
wish I could give a shout out to each of you personally but you know
who you are. Thank you and much love.

Adisa Salim

RAYNE

"Hello"

"Hello, where is Q?"

"Who?"

"Quest."

"Excuse me, who are you?"

"Who the hell are you and why are you answering my man's phone?"

"Your man?"

"YES!"

"How long have you known him?"

"We've been fucking for 6 months."

I had seen the picture of my husband's dick on his cell phone. His dumb ass had donated his old phone to the homeless shelter I volunteered at and failed to erase the pictures before handing it over. We give out old phones to the homeless because even if the phone doesn't have service or minutes it can still be used to call 911 in the event of an emergency. Luckily, I always go through any phones that are donated to the shelter to make sure the person didn't leave any phone numbers or pictures in it before I give the phones to residents. I almost didn't go through his phone, but thank God I did; because there it was, a picture of his manhood in all its glory. I had seen that thing up close and personal for 10 years so I knew it was him. When I questioned him about it, he claimed he was in the bathroom just playing around with the phone and snapped a picture. He was going to delete it but thought he might send it to me with a sexy message about what he planned to do to me when I got home; but he got busy and never did it. Yeah, right. He must think I'm Boo Boo, the fool. He wasn't even a good liar.

"Did he send you a picture of his dick?" I asked the strange woman on the other end of Quest's phone.

"No."

Before I could stop myself, I erupted in laughter. Of course, she wasn't the only woman my husband was fucking but I'm sure she thought she was. She was just one of many. With my husband, there was always some other woman. I couldn't even remember a time when he was faithful. I guess it's true, once a cheater, always a cheater.

4

"Do you use condoms?" I ask.

"No, why would I use a rubber with my man? I'm trying to get pregnant."

Now I'm laughing so hard, I can't speak. I'm waiting on Ashton Kutcher to jump from behind a building or a bush and tell me that I am being Punked. But this wasn't a practical joke. This woman was not a prank call from Uncle Tommy. This woman was screwing my husband raw and trying to get pregnant.

"Do you know who I am?" I asked the stranger.

"No." she replied, nonchalantly.

"I'm his wife."

"He told me he wasn't married."

"Well, stick around sweetie because he won't be for long." I hung up the phone and got my keys.

This was the story of my life…Once upon a time there was a boy and girl who loved each other than a slut came along and ruined everything. The End!

I was in my Hummer, driving and talking on the phone to my husband's latest mistress. I swerved around cars as I sped down I-65 toward his job. Enough was enough. There have always been other women and I have always forgiven him or turned a blind eye, but not this time. He was fucking her and didn't care enough about me to put a condom on? I don't understand men that will still play Russian roulette when it comes to sex.

I'm listening to my cheater playlist of Ceelo Green, "Fuck you" Blu Cantrell, "Hit em style" Rihanna, "Love the way you lie" Beyonce, "Irreplaceable" and Justin Timberlake, "Cry me a river". I am already in my feelings and know that this confrontation is not going to go well.

My gut was telling me to call him outside like I needed to see him and then run his ass over with my SUV. I practiced acting crazy while I was driving. I wondered if under the circumstances I could plead temporary insanity. It would be a crime of passion. Then again, I could plead it was self-defense because after all, his ass was trying to kill me by screwing different women without a condom. The shit made perfect sense to me. Hell, it should be a legitimate defense for the murder of cheating husbands everywhere.

I pulled up in front of the nightclub where my husband worked. Before, I could park and go inside, one of his friends had already ran inside and warned him that I was in the parking lot. He came outside looking like 50 shades of guilty.

"Who the hell is Mia?"

"What?"

"You heard me, who is Mia?"

"What?"

I felt like Samuel L. Jackson in Pulp Fiction. If this motherfucker says what one more time, I swear I'm going to shoot him on the spot.

"Stop playing dumb Quest or should I call you Q? I talked to her on the phone. She told me all about how she was fucking my husband raw; raw Quest? Really?"

"Baby, you know those girls just trying to come between us. They are just jealous. They want to be you. Don't let them jealous bitches mess up our good thing, baby."

"Stop lying. Do you think I am stupid? I've known about most the little tricks you mess with but I never said anything because I assumed you cared enough about me not to give me fucking AIDS, but you don't give a shit about your life or mine."

"Rayne, you know I wouldn't do no dumb shit like fuck a girl raw; the bitch is lying on me and you just going to believe what the hell she tells you. You are going to take some trick word over your own husband? That is so fucked up,"

"Stop it! It's bad enough you out here fucking around without a rubber but don't try to make out like you are the victim here. You are not going to turn this shit around on me."

"How many times do I have to tell you, I am not out there fucking around on you and if I did I would wear a rubber, Rayne, I love you. I wouldn't do that to you."

"Give me a condom."

"What?" There he goes with that what shit like he is hard of hearing.

"Reach in your pocket or your billfold or go in the backroom, wherever you keep your rubbers that you use when you cheat and give me one of them."

"I don't have any rubbers that would mean I was planning on cheating on you and I'm not."

He was such a fucking liar.

"Why are you asking me for a rubber, Rayne? See that's the shit I'm talking about right there. I'm trying to be honest with you and you trying to run games thinking you going to catch me up."

"Naw baby, I'm not trying to catch you up. I just thought I would see what is so great about fucking around. Since you love side pussy so much, I want to go get me some side dick."

Quest's whole demeanor changed immediately. I had never seen that look on his face and to be honest I never wanted to see it again. He stepped closer to me and grabbed my shoulder. When he spoke, his voice was louder even through clenched teeth.

"Rayne, don't play. If you ever let another man touch you I will kill you. I mean it. You are my wife."

"Get your hands off me." I shrugged his hands from my shoulder. "You should remember that I'm your wife when you out there fucking around."

We were starting to make a scene and people were gathering to watch. Black folks loved drama and mess and right now we were giving them plenty of both. Quest also noticed the crowd.

"Baby, we will talk about this when I get home tonight." He says in a lower tone.

I agreed to go home and wait for him so that we could finish our discussion.

The drive home had to be the longest ride I have ever taken. I was so tired of his bullshit. As much as I hated him and as mad as I was now, I knew a part of me could never let him go. He had this hold on me and he knew it. I'm going over our future conversation in my head. I am imagining myself telling him that I was leaving for good this time. I could hear him begging me to stay just like before. I had his apology memorized…

Baby, I'm sorry. I fucked up.

You know I love you.

I swear it will never happen again.

I just got caught up, baby.

I love you. You are my wife.

Those other women were just a piece of ass.

You got the ring.

I had heard that same apology countless times and each time he would say it I would forgive him. Over the past 10 years nothing had changed, not even his sorry ass apology. Insanity is repeating the same action and expecting a different result. I guess I'm past crazy because I keep forgiving Quest and each time, I think things will be different but they never are.

I never understood why women go after married men or continue seeing them after they find out the man is married. A married man cannot cheat unless a trifling woman allows him to do so. I wish women would start respecting other women and realize that we are the prize and not the cheating ass man. How could they think Quest was such a good man? If he was a good man, would he be cheating on me with them?

Quest

Fuck! Why can't these bitches ever stay in their fucking lane? You think I would have learned to pick better team players by now. Every time I think I got everything under control one of these tricks fuck up and does something stupid. Now I got to go home and try to smooth everything over with Rayne, again.

I should have never fucked Mia. I had made a huge mistake. The first rule of success is to not mix business and pleasure. I knew better. She had been my assistant but once sex entered the equation, she thought she had special privileges. Everything pretty much went to hell after that. She was always asking me when I was going to leave Rayne and marry her. That bitch had bumped her head. Why would I marry someone that had fucked at least two of my friends? You can't turn a hoe into a housewife. She had threatened to tell Rayne plenty of times but a good dick down and a few empty promises kept her quiet.

I have been caught so many times before but I managed to get my wife to forgive me. I knew sex made women vulnerable and even though she cried and fought against me, we would end up in bed and all would be forgiven. She would let me know, however, I was busted. Rayne didn't fly off the deep end like a lot of women. If she left she always came back. I never had to worry about Rayne cursing me out or busting the windows out of my car. She was too classy for that. No, what she did was subtler. There have been notes and pictures sent to Rayne or left on her car. Rayne would turn around and leave the same picture or note taped to the bathroom mirror where I couldn't miss it. If I didn't say anything about it neither would she. Most of the time I think she just wanted me to know that she knew.

Tonight, was different. She was mad. She wasn't playing. I almost expected her to be gone when I got home. Just the thought of Rayne leaving had me shook. I was sweating, breathing hard and generally feeling sick. I couldn't face her like this so I decided to go to my friend Baylor's house.

Baylor and I had been friends for a few years. We were complete opposites and folks always wondered why we were friends. I was the bad boy and Baylor was the good guy. I struggled all through school while Baylor graduated at the top of our class. I couldn't wait to be done with school and after I got my degree in Business, I never wanted to set foot in another classroom. Baylor loved school. He earned several degrees relating to engineering and computer programming. Baylor was shy and quiet while I was loud and sometimes obnoxious. We both got married right after college but while I was cheating before and after the nuptials, Baylor was happy to just have one woman. He wore his wedding band with pride and would quickly dismiss any woman that tried to entice him. He was strong where I was weak and that was our biggest difference.

I ring the doorbell and Baylor answers in his pajama pants and robe, looking like the Black Hugh Hefner. Even though I crack jokes about the way he dresses, my boy had style. We exchanged our normal pleasantries. He starts shaking his head and immediately turns to head toward the basement. His entire basement had been deemed the man cave. There were real arcade games lining the wall, fully stocked vending and soda machines that didn't take money, a pool table with personalized balls and a state-of-the art media center. He had a full bath, the most comfortable recliners, and a bar. My favorite part of the man cave was the virtual driving range that Baylor designed. I could come over and work on my golf swing while we talked.

"It's three in the morning so what's wrong Quest?" he asked, skipping all the formalities and getting right to the point.

"I fucked up, man."

"Damn boy, are you ever going to learn to keep your dick in your pants?"
I didn't need to tell Baylor what I had done wrong. He already knew whatever it was involved another woman.
I could tell Baylor was getting impatient with my repeated infidelities.

I went through the whole story about Rayne showing up at the club. Baylor listened intently; the only sound he made was a cluck of his tongue as he shook his head no. I knew in his mind he was already judging me. Baylor wouldn't cheat on his wife if a woman got butt naked on his bed with an arrow pointing to her pussy. I envied him for that.

"Quest, you got a good woman. Men would cut off a hand for the chance to be able to call her their wife but for some reason that is not good enough for you. Are you trying to end your marriage?"

10

"Hell no! I can't believe you would say that. You know I love Rayne, man. I can't imagine my life without her."

"Well you need to start imagining your life without her because that is going to eventually happen."

I felt that sick feeling come back to the pit of my stomach because I knew Baylor was right. Rayne was going to get tired one day and leave me. I knew it was just a matter of time.

"You are going to end up another victim of the 80-20 rule."

"Don't come at me with that Tyler Perry philosophical bullshit, Baylor, this is not the time."

"When would be the best time to bring it up, when Rayne is gone?"

I glared at Baylor. "I'm listening."

"I know you love Rayne. You are not cheating because you are missing something at home. There is something missing in you. You are selfish. You want to have your cake and eat it too. Cheating happens when you start looking for what you don't have or what you think you are missing. But faithfulness happens when you start thanking God for your blessings. You better realize what you have before you lose it."

As much as I didn't want to hear what Baylor was saying, he was telling the truth. I couldn't argue with him. I needed to go home and make things right with Rayne.

"I try to be faithful and I can do it for a while but it is like being an alcoholic. I can stay away from temptation for a while but then I fall off the wagon and back to my old ways. Every time I mess up, I can give Rayne an excuse or explain it away and she lets it go and we are back to being good."

Baylor shook his head again. "Every time you tell me another story about cheating, I think about Eddie Murphy's stand-up routine on Raw. Eddie talked about how a man got busted coming out of another woman's house and when she confronts him all he says is, "It wasn't me." Soon the woman starts to think maybe it wasn't him. She wants to believe him because what is the alternative? Leaving him? If she left him then the other woman wins and women are much too competitive for that. Rayne loves you enough that she forgives you and you keep taking her for granted."

I hate when Baylor starts lecturing me. I don't need a lecture. I could get that from Rayne. I just need a friend to listen and vent to

11

but I should have known it wouldn't be that simple with Baylor.

Baylor continues, "Eddie Murphy blames the denial phenomenon on good sex and a man's ability to make a woman say wooooo." We both laugh.

"You were Rayne's first and her only lover so she is attached to you mentally, emotionally and physically. But you are like Eddie Murphy's character in Boomerang. Woman bond to a man during sex. But as soon as you fuck a woman all the romance "skeets" out of you. The only woman that you weren't like that with was Rayne. That is how I knew she was the right one for you. Don't fuck this up, Q."

Baylor was right. I might as well bite the bullet and go home to face Rayne. Rayne stood out from other women because she refused to have sex until we got married. No matter how much I begged her when we were in high school and college she wouldn't give me any pussy. She would just say she was waiting until she got married. I thought when we got engaged she would give it up, but no, Rayne wouldn't budge.

"Engaged is not married." Rayne would tell me whenever I pressured her for sex.

"But we are going to get married, so what difference does it make now?"

"It makes a big difference to me." She insisted.

"Do you know how much pussy I could have had by now? Here I am trying to do right by you and you are just being selfish."

"Well, you can go get all the pussy you want Quest Harrison; just know this, if you do, then you will never get mine. The only man that will ever know what I feel like will be my husband, not my boyfriend but my husband."

"I am going to be your husband. You wouldn't buy a car without taking it on a test drive."

"I'm not a car."

I kept trying to leave her, thinking that if I did she would give in but it never worked. I always ended up begging for a second chance. Eventually I stopped pressuring her and told her that I would wait for her. I waited to have sex with Rayne but while I was waiting I was having sex with other women. After we got married, I just never stopped.

I know there is a difference for men between their actions before sleeping with a woman and after. A man can fuck and forget; a woman will fuck and follow. Rayne wasn't different from any other woman when it came to that, the only difference was I wanted her. Rayne doesn't understand that those other women don't mean anything to me but it's in their nature to want more from me. She is the only one I've ever loved. I guess I might as well bite the bullet and go home.

Rayne

I was young and inexperienced when Quest and I first got together. Quest was not my first boyfriend. No, my first boyfriend was Trent and I was 15 years old. Trent was dark chocolate but had hazel eyes. The contrast made him look beautifully exotic and I worshipped him. We had a lot in common. We grew up on the same block and we went to the same church. He was my friend long before he was my boyfriend. We spent most of our school day writing each other notes that we would slip through the metal grates of our lockers. We lived so close to the school that we walked home every day, holding hands and talking about our future. It was just puppy love at first but soon talk of sex was injected into our relationship and it pretty much went downhill. At the time, I was trying desperately to hold onto my virginity, so I would play around but didn't want to take it any further. Our sexual relationship was mostly kissing and grinding against each other with our clothes on. Eventually, I graduated to the occasional hand job with a generous amount of baby oil. Hand jobs satisfied him for a while but I always felt the pressure to have sex with him and it was getting to the point that it was becoming a real issue for us.

One day Trent brings up the topic of oral sex, which totally grossed me out. He tried everything to coax me into giving him some head but I flat out refused. He would pull his dick out and aim it towards my face. I would purse my lips together tightly and turn my head which didn't stop him from rubbing his dick against my cheek. If I wasn't ready to open my legs for him, I certainly wasn't going to open my mouth either.

He lived across the street from a woman that was in her early 20s and he started hanging at her house after school. We spent less and less time together because he was spending more and more time with her. I confronted him about his time with the neighbor.

"She likes to suck it and when I cum she swallows it. Are you going to do that? He asked.
I am completely disgusted by his revelation.

"I love you but I am not ready for that." Tears already running down my face.

Needless, to say he dumped me and I was heartbroken. I ended up running into him some years later. He had married his neighbor as soon as he was old enough. They had three children! I was still hurt and feeling some type of way over him dumping me. This fool had the nerve to approach me while sitting in his daddy van full of car seats. He didn't need to tell me how amazing I still looked. I knew it. I didn't want to hear about how much he missed me now. I had my Pretty Woman moment. You know when Julia Roberts went into a store and no one would wait on her, but she returned in designer clothes after an expensive shopping spree? That was me, I told him, he made a big mistake, HUGE! I not only gave head; I gave great head. I just needed him to be patient and work with me through the learning curve. But his loss was Quest's gain.

Quest came along when I was on the rebound from Trent. He was not the type I thought would ever take an interest in someone like me. He was a star athlete that played football, basketball and ran track. He had been voted homecoming king every year since the 10th grade. He was popular, sometimes too loud and always the center of attention.

I was shy, quiet and a bookworm that tried not to get noticed. I didn't participate in any extracurricular activities. I spent most of my time reading books and fantasizing that I was living the exciting life of some of those characters. I only had one friend, Corey Davis. Corey had mahogany colored skin, he was extremely short with glasses and braces and he followed me around the school like he was Eurkele and I was Laura. I guess because I was never mean to him we became best friends and our friendship has lasted till this day. Corey ended up being the ugly duckling that turned into a swan. By the time we graduated, he hit a growth spurt and ended up being 6'2, he lost the glasses and braces and even though he was handsome, I don't think he ever saw himself that way.

While I was trying to just get through high school and blend into the walls, Quest noticed me. At first I wouldn't talk to him and even when he asked for my phone number I refused to give it to him. I saw how he was with other girls at school and I didn't want to be another notch on his belt. I ignored him and the more I ignored him the harder he pursued me. I didn't give in until our senior year when he asked me to prom.

Here I was a little Miss Nobody and I was going to prom with Quest Harrison. Prom night was the first night I allowed him to kiss me. I had kissed Trent plenty of times before but Trent's kisses didn't have the same effect on me as Quest. When Quest kissed me, hot waterfall secretions flowed from my pussy wetting my lips and drenching my panties.

It didn't take long before we became a couple but I still refused to have sex with him. My virginity meant something to me and I was going to save myself for my husband. Quest was used to women opening their legs for him but I refused. He even tried pressuring me into sex by breaking up with me but I held my ground. I was not losing my virginity and if it meant losing him then I would just have to live with that.

Quest married me right after we graduated from college. He had been the first and only man I had been with. I had no desire to have sex with any man other than my husband but Quest still treated women like they were on an all-you-can-eat-buffet. He cheated before and after we got married. I thought once we said our vows things would be different. The only difference was he also got to fuck me, the only woman that had ever told him no.

By the time I got home from confronting Quest about his latest affair, I was exhausted. My eyes were heavy and my head was throbbing. I went to the bathroom and turned the water on in the tub. When I got in the tub I thought about my conversation with Quest at the club. I had never seen that side of Quest and as much as it scared me, it excited me too. It's sad that the most passion I got from him was when I threatened to go fuck another man. I wondered could I fuck another man. Did I have it in me to cheat? What would Quest do if he found out that I had cheated?

I slid down into the tub and closed my eyes. I tried to fantasize about my mystery man but all I could see was Quest, watching me, with that look he gave me at the club. How could I cheat when I can't even imagine being with another man? Quest was my first and only lover. Instead of fantasizing about an affair with a mystery man, I dreamed about Quest and how he would react if he thought I was fucking another man.

I see Quest walk in as I am kissing the stranger. He is so angry that he knocks the other man out with one punch. I am trembling with fear. He walks over to me and slaps me in the face. Hard! I fall to the ground and begin sobbing from the sting on my cheek. He picks me up from the floor and starts ripping my clothes off.

"Is this what you want; another man's hands all over you? You want to be treated like a slut, then that is how I'm going to treat you."

Quest is angry and rough. He is not making love to me, not tonight. My clothes are in shreds on the floor where he ripped them off my body. He grabs me by my hair and forces me to my knees.

"Open your mouth." He growls instructions. I comply. Still holding my hair, he guides his dick into my mouth. He is fucking my mouth with such force that I must hold on to his thighs to steady myself. My free hand is between my legs rubbing my clit.

"You like being treating like a whore, don't you? Yes, you do. You like for me to fuck your mouth. I bet your pussy is super wet from having this dick down your throat. Let me see?"

He pushes me further down so that I am on all fours.

He kneels beside me and shoves one finger in my pussy.

"See, I knew you would be wet. Sucking a dick always makes a nasty bitch wet."

He shoves another finger in my pussy and then another. Within minutes I am cumming so hard I'm about to pass out.

I withdraw my fingers from my pussy and get out of the tub. Damn, I wish I could experience that type of passion with Quest in real life. Our real-life sex was a bit boring. We didn't experiment and we didn't do any of the nasty stuff that I read about in books and saw on the videos he kept in his home office. He taught me how to give him a proper blow job and of course he ate my pussy but our sex life was the same routine. He wouldn't do any of those freaky things with me but he would cheat and do them with random women in the streets. I understand that I was a virgin when we got married but once we got married it should be ok for us to do any and everything together.

I fell asleep almost as soon as I got in the bed. I didn't hear Quest when he came in, but I saw the evidence that he was home. There was a bouquet of flowers, red roses, on the dresser. I picked up the card that was attached to the flowers and read it.

It said: *To Rayne, my wife for life.*

Wow, I bet it took him all night to come up with that. I looked at the flowers again and shook my head. After 10 years of marriage, he either doesn't know or doesn't care that my favorite flower is a tulip. I hate roses. Beside the flowers was a card. I walked over and picked up the card. I didn't bother to read the outside but opened it to read what he had written. It was his apology; the same apology that I had heard countless times before. I walked over to the closet and got out my suitcase. I was leaving this time. With trembling hands, I picked up my suitcase and went to the dresser. I opened the drawer and looked down at my underwear. Pretty bras and lacy panties were all folded the exact same way and lined up perfectly; neat and organized. I loved organization. I craved routine. I didn't like change. I knew it and he knew it. Who was I kidding? Where would I go if I left? What would I do? He was all I had, all I've ever known.

 I closed my suitcase and put it back in the closet. I walked in the living room and found Quest asleep on the couch.
Despite everything I still loved this man with every fiber of my being. I know I'm a good woman, I just wish I could get some do right out of him. Shaking my head, I walked into the kitchen and began to pull out pans so that I could cook breakfast. This was a part of our routine, too. No matter what, I had cooked this man's breakfast every morning for the past 10 years.

 We normally listened to music while we ate and in my passive aggressive way, I got to tell him how I felt. I had a soundtrack of Betty Wright, Mary J, Kelly Prince, Alicia, Whitney and some R. Kelly. Because no man understands more about a woman being fed up then my boy Robert. This morning we were listening to *"It's a thin line between love and hate."* His dumb ass sang along with the music unfazed by the lyrics. Honestly, listening to him sing the words to that song was starting to piss me off.

THE SWEETEST WOMAN IN THE WORLD
COULD BE THE MEANEST WOMAN IN THE WORLD
IF YOU MAKE HER THAT WAY
YOU KEEP HURTING HER
SHE'LL KEEP BEING QUIET
SHE MIGHT BE HOLDING SOMETHING INSIDE
THAT'LL REALLY, REALLY, HURT YOU ONE DAY
THERE'S A THIN LINE BETWEEN LOVE AND HATE

 Yes, He was sitting there, singing away, while I'm standing behind him, stirring a big ole pot of grits with cheese. I imagined pouring those delicious, bubbly hot grits all down his back. Just the thought was enough to make me smile.

The sad part was this wasn't close to the first time that I caught Quest cheating. The first time I caught Quest cheating was when I left for work but came home early because I wasn't feeling well. I pulled into the driveway and I was a little surprised to see Quest's car; but, it wasn't unusual for him to come home to pick up a contract or even to sneak in a power nap. I tried being extra quiet as I entered the house in case he was sleeping.

As I walked up the stairs, I heard grunting and groaning in my husband's baritone voice. The bedroom door was wide open so I could walk into my bedroom quietly and unnoticed. Clothing had been hastily discarded all around the room. My naked husband was fucking some woman with a huge ass doggie style in our bed.

I stood there watching as he was pulling her honey blond hair with one hand like the reins on a horse while slapping her ass with the other one. He was in a rhythm. His pelvis thrusting forward as her huge ass came crashing back against him.

"Is it good to you, Daddy?" The woman with the big ass asked my husband.

"Hell yes, I love fucking you. I knew you had some good pussy." Quest replied, his voice laden with lust. "I wanted that pussy as soon as you walked in the club."

"Spank my ass, Daddy," she begged.
Slap! Slap! He obliged.

Quest held her by the hip with one hand and used the other hand to slap the woman's ass. I watched as each time he lifted his hand to strike her ass the muscles across his back rippled. I had never seen this side of Quest. Come to think of it, I never saw Quest during sex. Sex was something we did in the dark and even then, my eyes were closed. I didn't want to see him making love to another woman but I couldn't turn away either.

"Yes, I love it, again. Harder!" The woman's scream intensified.
Slap! Slap!

The sound of my husband's hands striking her flesh echoed in our bedroom. I wanted to scream. I wanted to run away but I couldn't. It might seem weird but I wanted to watch. Quest was fucking in a way that I had never seen before. He was forceful and almost angry. He was not the same tender and loving man that had just made love to me the night before.

The muscles in his back rippled every time he drew his hand back to strike her ass. With every blow, she screamed with pleasure and asked for more. Quest's hand was slightly cupped and his hand striking her ass made this sound. It's hard to describe the sound but for some reason that sound of hand slapping naked flesh and the way they talked to each other was having an unexpected effect on me; I was turned on.

They were both so caught up that neither of them noticed me. I walked closer to the bed. I wanted to see their faces. I needed to see if he was enjoying sex with her more than he enjoyed sex with me. I walked up to the bed and looked at my husband's face. He was lost in the feeling. His eyes were closed and his bottom lip was clenched between his teeth. I watched the rise and fall of his chest and his nostrils flare with each stroke. Their fucking became more feverish and just as he was about to get off I tapped him on the shoulder.

"Oh, Fuck!" Quest yelled.

I don't know if his reaction was from being caught or because he was cumming and couldn't stop his nut from shooting all over the woman's legs and the comforter my mother gave us. The woman jumped out of the bed, pulling the sheet around her to cover up her nakedness. I almost laughed. What the hell was she trying to cover up? I had already seen everything God and her plastic surgeon had given her. I wanted to grab her, drag her down the stairs and beat her ass on my perfectly manicured lawn. I surprised by my calmness.

Quest was trying to put his draws on and explain that I didn't see what I saw. I had just caught him with another woman in our bed and the best excuse he could give me was, it wasn't me? I walked down the stairs, grabbed my purse and walked out the front door. Quest was running behind me still giving me lame ass excuses as I got in my car and drove away. It wasn't until I was out of his sight that the tears started to fall. I wasn't even mad at him. I was hurt. It wasn't about the cheating it was what I saw. He was enjoying that woman in a way he has never been with me. I pulled over and cried on the side of the road before driving to my mom's house.

I stayed gone for about a week before my husband convinced me to forgive him and come back home. Everything was great. He was attentive and loving but that is how it always is once he is caught doing wrong. Whenever he gets caught he becomes Mr. Super Husband. But I had grown tired of the games. I was tired of the lies and the cheating. Shit, sometimes you should give up on people. It's not because you don't care, but because they don't.

Giselle

One of these days, I am going to write the memoirs of my life. I can already see it on the big screen. I've often thought about who in Hollywood was fabulous enough to portray me. My first choice would probably be Halle Berry. She was pretty enough but Miss Thing was just skin and bones. Honey, I was voluptuous. Perfect DD breast and an ass that you could sit a serving tray on. Then again you know through movie magic and make up they turned the beautiful Charlize Theron into an ugly ass, trailer park serial killer; so, anything was possible.

My story would probably start like Steve Martin's monologue in the movie, *The Jerk*. He was born a little White boy in an all-Black family. Well me, child, I was born a little Black boy named Jeffery in a conservative Christian family but I later transformed into the Goddess Giselle Armani; the house mother of the Armani family.

I came from an affluent Atlanta family and my parents had high hopes for their only son. I excelled in sports and made good grades. I was a good-looking young man. But ever since I was old enough to look in a mirror, I knew the person looking back at me was not the person that I was inside. My outside was all boy but I knew with every fiber of my being that I was a girl. I know people don't believe that homosexuals are born gay, people think it's a choice but who in their right mind would choose to live like this? I would never choose to have my father hate me. My father made it clear that he would never accept me as being anything other than a heterosexual man. If we were out and saw a gay man, my father would tell me that I better not ever, ever even think about bringing that disgusting immoral shit to his house. He would rather have a dead son then a gay son.

It wasn't until I went off to college that I was brave enough to start the journey into discovering who I was meant to be. What I wanted more than anything was for my insides and my outsides to match. Being a broke college student, I didn't have money to start hormones and lacked the funds for plastic surgery so I became a male escort. I couldn't believe how much money I made by entertaining old White men that loved being fucked by a well-endowed Black man. I dropped out of college and stacked my paper. Not only did they pay a pretty penny for my company, they also splurged on expensive gifts for me. The best trick I had was a well-known plastic surgeon. Honey, he changed my life. I was on my way to getting the injections in back rooms by shady folks trying to take advantage of those that are desperate to change their appearance. Thankfully, the old doctor hooked me up. I could get cheek implants, my Adam's apple shaved, breast implants, and butt injections. When it came down to the final surgery, turning my dick into a pussy, I was hesitant. Even though I knew as a woman, I should have the surgery to create a pussy, my dick was my bread and butter.

I took some of the money that I saved and opened Atlanta's trendiest gay club, The Rainbow Room. The club was booming and my money troubles were a thing of the past. I could stop tricking and be legit. It also gave me a chance to find true love.

My husband, Egypt, was a singer and played the guitar. He reminded me of Lenny Kravitz, when he was going through his dreadlocked, grunge phase. He was cool and serene and had this very mellow vibe that drew people to him. He was one of the most spiritual people I knew. After meeting him, Christianity became a part of my past. He enlightened me to not only the world around me but he helped me to define my own identity.

Egypt told me in the beginning of creation that there were no men only women. Honey, I had a complete come-apart when he told me that. I grew up believing that humanity started with Adam so to say we all came from a woman was blasphemous. He said that all embryos started as female and that is why men have nipple even though they can't breastfeed. Due to genetic mutations, the clit will enlarge and become a dick and the ovaries will drop down and become testicles. He claimed that this was the real "fall of man." I had to let go of my Christian ideology to be open to what he was saying. Of course, my Daddy would completely disagree with Egypt's logic. He would tell me God made Adam and Eve, not Adam and Steve. He would insist Adam came first and Eve was created from his rib and anything else was immoral and unnatural. If Egypt's logic doesn't seem reasonable then how could a dust man and a rib woman make sense to anyone? I finally realized that anyone that believes in talking snakes and a pregnant virgin has no right to call me unnatural.

Egypt was such a free spirit. He loved everyone. It used to piss me off when his mulatto ass would say shit like he didn't see color. The world sees color and feels the need to remind people of it.

Being Black was part of who I was so if a person doesn't see my color then they don't see me. He told me that we are all from the continent known as Africa, the separation by color just keeps humans divided. We all need each other.

God, that man is beautiful, inside and out. I know that is why everyone loves him. People would travel from all over to see him perform. He performed all over Atlanta but not just in trendy nightclubs and hot spots; he performed on street corners. He is one of those musicians that cares more about his artistic expression then about making money. I tried to go to as many gigs as possible but it's hard when I must look after my own club.

Tonight, I would get to see him in action. He was performing at a nightclub that was Atlanta's version of the Apollo. If you were true about your craft, then you had to be tested by fire in front of the Diamond crowd. The Diamond Den was a fabulously delicious club that was often frequented by Atlanta's elite.

Egypt and I arrived early so that we could enjoy a nice dinner before he had to get ready to hit the stage. Our schedules didn't allow us to spend a lot of time out on the town so tonight was a special treat. Egypt is a complete vegan which means that I'm pretty much a vegetarian, at least in front of him. Egypt said that animals deserve to live and that we were put here to look over and protect the earth. He was such a sensitive soul.

Egypt took it upon himself to order for us. I used to get so irritated when he would do that but now I love it. I love how he took charge and how he took care of me. Plus, if I ordered, my food would come with a dead animal. Egypt started us off with butternut squash soup with crispy shiitake mushrooms and chives. We followed the soup with an entrée of vegetables and pasta sautéed with garlic and tomato-basil sauce. After we finished eating, Egypt excused himself to go warm up and I found a seat at the bar to enjoy the opening acts. I saw a very good looking man walking towards me with a big smile on his face. Out of all the empty bar seats available, why this fool wants to sit right next to me?

"Are you enjoying yourself?" The man with the 100-watt smile asked me.

I sighed, "It's ok."

"Well ma'am, ok is not good enough for me. What would make your experience exceptional?"

"Why do you care?" I questioned, Mr. Charming.

"Because I am the owner of this here fine establishment and I can't afford to have you out there bad mouthing my spot to all your girlfriends and stuff. By the way, my name is Quest and you are?"

"I am Giselle" I say, finally giving him a half-hearted smile.

"Miss Giselle what are you drinking on? Whatever you want. I got you." Quest says and put his hand much too high on my thigh.

"Right now what I need more than a drink is a place to relieve myself of the drinks I have already had."

"I was on my way to the little boy's room myself. I would gladly escort you to the ladies' room if you don't mind."

He extends his arm and I intertwine mine around his muscular bicep.

When we get to the restrooms, Quest takes a bow before going into the men's room.

I was about to go into the women's bathroom but security was standing there and using a bathroom that is different from the gender on your birth certificate could land a person in jail for 6 months. I went into the men's room and Quest was at the urinal. He had his head back and his eyes closed while relieving himself. He didn't even see me when I stood beside him. I hiked up my dress and started urinating.

"What's up, bro." Quest said as he opened his eyes and turned his head to face me.

"What the fuck! What the fuck are you doing? You're a man?" He looked just as puzzled as he was angry.

I finished peeing and adjusted my clothing to leave when Quest felt the need to call me a faggot.

"Yes, and I must be a good one since I had you craving a taste of my good wood." I said as I blew Quest a kiss.

The first punch grazed my cheek. It wasn't hard enough to do damage but it was enough to piss me off.

I took the heel of my palm and jabbed it right between his eyes. It was on then. We started trading blow for blow until we fell against the door and out the bathroom. I landed on my back and Quest was on top me. The off-duty police officer separated us then slapped on handcuff before putting me in his squad car.

Egypt was backstage so he had no idea that I was on my way to jail. He wouldn't even know I was missing until he got home after his show. Counting on him to bail me out would have meant staying locked up longer than necessary. Not only did I not want to be there, I needed to get back to check on the Rainbow Room. As soon as I was processed in to the Fulton County Jail, I called the most responsible and dependable child of the Armani family, a stud named Lee.

Lee was my pride and joy. He was successful, sweet and he loved Mother Giselle. It seemed like I was always bailing my other house children out of all types of trouble, paying bills and giving them a place to stay, but Lee had his act together. I could see his concern when he saw my bruised faced.

"Child, don't you worry about Mother. If you think I look bad you should see the other guy." I try to joke to lighten the mood.

"You should press charges against whoever did this to you. Don't let them get away with putting their hands on you." Lee was pissed.

"Trust me, I'm fine. Besides I think he learned his lesson tonight. Don't let this pretty face and this fine ass body fool you. Not only do I slay, but I'll slay any bitch that thinks he is going to put his hands on me, boom!!" I emphasize my meaning with a snap of my fingers.

"Come on, I was on my way to the Rainbow Room. I could use a drink."

"First, take me home so I can get myself fixed up. You know I can't be seen looking like I just stepped out of the Thriller video."

Baylor

People who know me now would never guess how rough I grew up. The Baylor of today is a far cry from the Baylor that grew up on the Southside of Chicago. We lived in a rough neighborhood. I was the only boy in a family with 4 girls. My daddy had walked out on my mom when she was pregnant with me. My sister's dads had abandoned them as well. We grew up hard and poor. Most kids that come from where we come from don't survive their teens. Attending a teenager's funeral was more likely than their graduation. If they weren't murdered, then they become drug addicts or dealers. There was a cycle of dependence on public housing and the standard proof of making it in my hood was when a teenage mother could move out of her mother's project into her very own. I was always determined to make my way out. I was born in that environment but I refused to be a product of it.

My mom always worried about me growing up in a house full of women. She thought it made me too soft, too weak and in our neighborhood, that could be deadly. Often she would send me to stay with her brother, James. We all called James, Uncle Joe. His job was to make a man of me, to teach me and do all the father-son things my deadbeat dad wasn't around to do. Uncle Joe had retired from the Army as a Warrant officer. He taught Junior ROTC at a local high school. He was a great teacher and basketball coach and all the kids referred to him as Chief. Financially, he was much better off than my mom. Besides he didn't have any kids of his own and had just divorced his third wife. So, when my mom asked him if he could take me in, he agreed. After all, I was his only nephew and every boy needed a male role model.

Staying with Uncle Joe was great. I didn't have to share a room with my sisters. The school was much nicer and Uncle Joe spoiled me with name brand clothes and shoes. There was always plenty to eat at his house. I settled into my life with Uncle Joe and I became an excellent student. I had a plan. I knew the key to never living like my mom was to go to college and since there was no money for tuition, I would have to excel so that I could get scholarships to cover my entire college ride.

Life in the suburbs beat the hell of the ghetto any day. Everything was perfect until I turned 12 years old. I was soaking in the tub when Uncle Joe walked into the bathroom. At first he apologized for busting in on me but he didn't leave back out. Instead he walked over to the tub and sat on the edge. I felt uneasy but this was Uncle Joe, he had rescued me from a horrible situation.

"Hey buddy, give me the towel and let me wash your back."

"I got it Uncle Joe, thanks." I say, still feeling uneasy but not wanting to offend the only person that had ever helped me.

"Boy, give me that towel. It isn't like you have something that I haven't seen before. I changed your diaper when you were baby. Stop acting shy and let me wash your back."

I hand Uncle Joe the towel and he starts washing my back. Washing my back didn't make me feel that uncomfortable it was when he started washing my lower back and would take the towel and rub it under my butt.

"Ok, thanks Uncle Joe. I got it from here." I said.

"Boy don't be silly. This towel is filthy so you haven't been doing a good job at bathing yourself so I'm going to have to do it for you. Now stand up."

"I got it Uncle Joe, I'll make sure I do a good job." I insist.

"I said stand your ass up, now." Uncle Joe was serious and I had never heard him use such a stern tone.

I stand up in front of Uncle Joe. My back is to him. I hear him dip the towel in the water and he stands up behind me and begins to wash my back again. This time though he doesn't stop at my back he takes the towel and washes my bottom.

"I don't like this Uncle Joe. Please stop." My voice is small and shaking. Tears are falling from my eyes, sliding down my cheeks and landing on my chest. I am scared.

"You don't tell me to stop when I'm buying you things and taking you places. You didn't tell me to stop when I took you in and did everything for you that your mama and daddy couldn't do, but now you want me to stop. You can pack your shit and leave tonight. Hell, your mama doesn't even want you back. You are going to end up in one of those group homes where they barely feed you." Uncle Joe was angry. I had never heard him talk like this before. He was usually so nice to me. I was scared. He stood up and threw the towel in the bathwater.

"I'm sorry." I said, bowing my head.
He paused at the door, his right hand on the doorknob.

"That is much better." He said, turning around slowly to face me again. "You know everything I do for you and to you is only because I love you. But you can't tell anyone about this or they will take you from me and put you in one of those homes for real. This has to be our secret ok?"

"Ok, I won't tell anybody, Uncle Joe." I submit.

"Good boy, now turn around." Uncle Joe instructed and I obeyed.

Uncle Joe puts his mouth on my private area. This was not right. I am crying and scared but Uncle Joe doesn't care. He continued sucking until he brings me to my first orgasm.

"See, I knew you would like it." He said before he standing up to leave.

"Don't forget this is our secret." He reminded me.

"Yes sir, I won't tell." I continue crying.

I must have sat in that tub for an hour. I didn't know what to think and couldn't make sense of what had just happened. I thought I did something wrong. I felt guilty and ashamed but mostly just confused. I finally got of the tub and went to my room. For a minute the thought crossed my mind that I should tell my mom, my teacher or somebody. Instead, I locked my bedroom door and cried myself to sleep because deep down, I knew that even if someone believed me, no one would care.

Over the years, Uncle Joe became more aggressive in his molestation, graduating from performing oral sex on me to making me perform it on him. It didn't take long before he started to sodomize me on a regular basis. I hated him. I thought about taking one of the many guns he kept in the house and blowing his brains out but I knew prison was not where I wanted to spend my life. I just kept telling myself this is temporary. I worked twice as hard as anyone else in school and graduated Valedictorian. I chose to attend Tuskegee University to continue my education, not only because they had one of the best engineering programs but also to get as far away from my childhood home and memories as possible. I left and never looked back. Uncle Joe never tried to contact me after I left. If he had I probably would have killed him.

There was one time, right before my 17th birthday that I tried telling my mom what my Uncle did to me. She told me I was lying and that I was ungrateful and just plain wrong to accuse my Uncle of such horrible things when all he had ever done was be nice and take care of me. I never spoke to my mom again after that day. I learned that sometimes you must give up on people, not because you don't care, but because they don't. I learned to keep quiet. I learned that just because someone shares genetics with you it doesn't make them your family. Rejection is an opportunity for your selection. I didn't have a choice about who shared my blood but from now on I would choose who I called family.

Rayne

It didn't take long for my intuition to pick up the Quest-is-cheating-again vibe. The signs are always the same. He becomes attached to the hip to all his electronic devices, phones, IPad, and laptop. Everything was password protected and never left his sight. I knew of a few hook-up sites he had been on before he started putting passwords on everything. I decided I would go on those sites and create fake profiles.

I went on Black People Meet, Badoo, Tinder, POF, AFF and Fling and created profiles. I also put one on a site called, Ashley Madison. Ashley Madison was an online dating service that was marketed toward people who were married or in committed relationships. Their slogan is "Life is short, have an affair." This was the perfect site for my husband so I created a fake profile with pictures of a woman I knew was his type. He liked Black women with a lighter complexion, she couldn't be skinny because he loved a fat ass and thick thighs. She also had to have big pretty lips. He was a sucker for pretty lips and pretty feet. Oh yes, he had a major foot fetish. I thought it was a little weird at first, his obsession with my feet. But I learned to accept it.

My first experience with his foot fetish was when we went on vacation to Pigeon, Tennessee. We stayed in a little cabin called Paradise Point, a beautiful place with a spectacular view, Jacuzzi and a fireplace. We were soaking in the hot tub and he was massaging my feet. It felt so good and I was so relaxed that I dozed off. When I opened my eyes, my husband had both of my feet wrapped around his dick like a cup and he was using my feet to jack off. My startled look must have startled him because he stopped. I didn't want him to feel bad like I thought he was a freak or something, so I put my feet back on his dick and he got hard again. When we moved from the hot tub to the bed he showed his love of feet. They had to touch him the entire time. He had them on his chest, toes in his mouth. Both in his hands, rubbing them as we fucked. He worshipped my feet. Once I knew how much my feet turned him on, I always made sure I kept my feet on point. I only wore open toe shoes when it was warm and if I wanted to get him going I would ask for a foot massage. Hell, to each his own, who am I to judge.

I finish creating my profile. My screen name was want2callUdaddy and the about me section read:

I am new to this site. I've never done anything like this before. I love my husband but I am just not sexually fulfilled. I am looking for a man that knows how to eat pussy. I want a man to fuck me until I can't walk. My hot spot are my feet, suck on my toes and you will make me squirt. No strings attached, I just want to have fun.

Now that my profile was created, I began to search through the profiles of the men on the site. While I am browsing, I get a message alert. Within an hour of creating my profile, I had a message from Quest whose screen name was pussypleaser. My blood began to boil but I was going to keep my cool.

Pussypleaser:
Hello, I'm Quest. How are you? The message popped up on my computer screen.

Want2callUdaddy:
I'm Nia, Nice to meet you Quest.

Pussypleaser:
First, let me ask this and just gone and get it out the way. Were you born a female? Do you have the vagina God gave you or the one a doctor gave you?

Want2callUdaddy:
I am a natural born woman

Pussypleaser:
Ok, so what brings a beautiful woman like you to a site like this? I know you don't have any trouble finding a man that would be willing to make love to you.

Want2callUdaddy:
The thought of the complete anonymity of online dating appeals to me. I can meet a stranger and based solely on the way he looks in a picture; I can pick him, meet him and have sex with no fear of judgement.

Pussypleaser:
So, have you ever done anything like this before?

Want2callUdaddy:
No, this is my first time. I've never cheated before but I am so unhappy and unsatisfied with my sex life at home with my husband. So why are you cheating on your girlfriend or are you married too?

Pussypleaser:

32

I'm married and no I've never cheated on my wife before. I would have never cheated on her but she is sick and not able to have sex. She didn't want me to be lonely and she knew I had needs that she could no longer fulfill, so she told me to find someone that could give me what she could no longer do.

I almost came out of character. Did this motherfucker just lie that I was sick and couldn't fuck anymore? I had to walk away from my laptop for a minute to calm down. I'm pacing back and forth looking at his lies on the computer screen. I'm holding a monologue in my head and I'm trying to talk myself off the ledge. I got this. I sit back down and start typing again.

Want2callUdaddy:
I'm sorry to hear about your wife. I know that must be rough on you.

Pussypleaser:
Yes, it has been and I feel guilty for wanting to meet someone. I feel like all my time should be spent caring for her but I just miss the touch of a woman. Am I wrong for that?

Want2callUdaddy:
Of course not, I feel a connection with you and I think we can help heal each other, if you are interested.

My hands stab roughly with each keystroke I type.

Pussypleaser:
Yes, in fact, I am free today if you are? I know this hotel right outside the city limits. It's secluded and cozy and we can take our time and enjoy exploring each other's body. I'm sure I can give you what you need.

I bet you can, you lying, cheating bastard, I think to myself but I type...

Want2callUdaddy:
That sounds wonderful.

Pussypleaser:
Do you have a number where I can contact you?

Shit! I didn't think that far ahead. I couldn't give him my number or he would know it's me. Fuck!! Ok, think, Rayne. I gave him the first number that popped in my head, my best friend, Corey. STUPID!!!! If he calls the number a man is going to answer or if it goes to voicemail, then he will hear a male voice. I convinced Quest that I was using my husband's old phone and he still had access to it I explained that I had to be careful about receiving phone calls and

33

text messages. I told him that when he got the room to text me with a message that says, this is KeKe, give me a call at 706-734-2 and let the last three numbers be the room number. So, that way if my husband looks at the messages he will not get suspicious.

Ok, he types back, I am heading over there now. See you in a little bit.

I can't wait, I reply back.
I log off and call my friend Corey. I explain to him that I just gave Quest his number.

"Why would you give your husband my number?"

"I made a fake profile to catch him cheating and when he asked for my number I panicked. Your number was the first one that I thought of." I explained.

"Rayne, I don't want to get caught up in the middle of whatever mess you and Quest got going on."

"You won't. I promise. I just need this favor from you. Please." I beg.

"Ok, what am I supposed to do when he calls me? I can't change the tone of my voice to pass as a female."

"You don't have to. I told him that the phone I was using was my husband's phone and he still had access to it so I had to be careful. He is going to text you as KeKe. Just forward me his text message."

I could hear the sigh of irritation through the phone and I knew Corey was shaking his head and rolling his eyes. He had told me a dozen times to leave Quest. Every time I would come crying to him, he would tell me not to go back and like a fool I always did. I know he didn't want to get involved because he knew just like the other times, I would never leave, at least not for good.

"Ok, Rayne. I'll do it."

"Thank you, Thank you. I owe you one."

We hung up the phone and I jumped in the shower. If I was going to be my husband's fake future mistress, then I needed to look the part. I put on a black pencil skirt that hugged my curvy hips in all the right places and a crisp white blouse with a low plunging neckline. I admired my ample cleavage in the mirror. As I slipped on my sleek black stiletto pumps, I thought to myself, why am I not enough for him? I know I wasn't experienced in sex when we got married but I was open-minded and willing to try anything. Quest was the one that said he always wanted me to act like a lady, in and out of the bedroom. Why would he tell me that but go and fuck some of the trashiest women on the planet?

I finished my make-up and pulled my hair back into a bun. I put on small gold hoop earrings and gave myself a final look in the mirror before heading out of the door. As I drove down the road, I had no plan on what I was going to do once I got to the hotel. I was completely winging it. I go to the second floor of the hotel and find room 215. I was about to knock on the door but then I thought, if I knock on this door then Quest is going to look through the peephole and know it's me and not open the door. I stand on the side of the door and text Corey. I asked him to text my husband and say that I am in the lobby and since this is our first time meeting I would feel safer if he came down to get me. People would see us together instead of me just walking into his room.

Corey text my husband and then text me back that he said ok. I hear movement coming from the other side of the door so I position myself as close to the door as possible. The door knob turns, the door opens, and there is my husband. As soon as he sees me he freezes. Neither of us speak. We just stare at each other. He doesn't try to explain. He doesn't try to shut the door. We both just stand there looking at each other for what felt like hours. Finally, I break the silence and speak first.

"Hello, Quest." I say in my normal tone.

"Rayne." Is his only reply to me.

I push my way past him and walk into his room. He had outdone himself this time. He had the suite with the Jacuzzi tub. Wine was chilling on ice; a bouquet of red roses lies beside a tall honey colored candle and there on the night stand was the biggest fucking box of condoms I have ever seen. Oh, he had big plans for his rendezvous.

I walked into the bathroom and it was obvious that he had already showered. He must have stopped by the store and picked up some body wash and deodorant. He wised up from the other times he got caught cheating. You can't leave home smelling like Zest and come home smelling like Caress.

I was too tired to fight. Too sick of excuses to stand around and listen. I was sick and tired of being sick and tired. This time I was done. I didn't say a word to Quest. I walked over to the dresser and picked up his keys. After taking the key to the house off his key chain, I walked out of the hotel and got in my car. I felt the tears start to sting my eyes but I refused to shed another tear over this no good, cheating ass man. I closed my eyes and dared a tear to fall. Not today! Before I could start my car, my cell phone rings. It's Quest, so I send it straight to voicemail.

He sends me a text.

Baby, I am so sorry that I attempted to cheat on you. I don't have an excuse. What I did was wrong and I'm sorry. I know I don't deserve a woman like you but I love you. I am sorry I keep fucking up but I will go to counseling or whatever you want to do. Please, just give me one more chance.

I feel defeated. I don't know why I keep trying to catch him because when I do nothing changes. Once a cheater always a cheater and by forgiving him all I was doing was enabling him and I needed to stop.

Quest

Part of me should have known that the woman I met online was a set-up. It was just too fucking easy but I was thinking with my dick and not my head, again. Fuck, I could have shit a brick when I opened the door and Rayne was standing there. I just stood there looking and feeling like an ass and all Rayne did was look at me and shake her head like she was trying to wake herself up from a bad dream.

I knew I had fucked up when she didn't say anything. She didn't ask any questions. She didn't want an explanation. She walked in the room and took the house key off my keychain and left. She had never done that before. Damnit! Maybe this was the last straw. What if she had reached that breaking point? I had pushed my luck one time too many. I thought I would just give her a chance to calm down before I came home. We had worked through our problems before and I'm sure we could work through it this time. I just had to let her get over her initial emotions. Fuck, Baylor was right. Maybe I have an addiction because there was no way to explain why I would keep chasing ass when I had a great woman at home.

As bad as I had fucked up, I though since I already had the room I might as well call someone to come over and keep me company. Jade was a bisexual chic that I hooked up with from time to time. She was a pretty chocolate girl with a Nick Minaj ass. She was a team player. I could call her and she was always ready. She didn't cause me any problems. She wasn't trying to be wifey. I met her when she was young and needed help financially. We worked out a deal where I helped her out occasionally with cash and she hooked me up with some of the best pussy and head I ever had.

I made the call and within an hour she was knocking on my hotel room door, wearing a barely-there dress. She didn't require coaxing or conversation. She walked in the room and got naked immediately. She crawled up from the foot of the bed between my legs and put my dick in her mouth. She always looked at me when she gave me head like she had to see my approval. She loved to see the expression of pleasure on my face and I loved her sloppy head, all the spitting, slurping, and slobbering. It didn't take long before she had sucked me completely dry. I was going to return the favor but she said she was good.

"I have a man now and he can tell if someone else has been in his cookie jar. "Jade said while getting dressed.

"I appreciate you. I am really stressed and you know how to relax a brother."

"Anytime baby." She blew me a kiss as she walked out and closed the door behind her.

Damn, I was feeling good and relaxed. I would just stay here and wait for Rayne to want me to come back home. She never stayed mad for long.

Lee

      I met Rayne one night when she accidentally stumbled into the Rainbow Room. The Rainbow Room was a gay club and it was magnificent and beautifully decorated. The waitresses wore outfits that reminded me of showgirls in Vegas. They wore rainbow striped corsets and tiny black ruffled bottoms. Rayne walked in and sat alone at the bistro style table meant for two. She looked hurt and lonely. The minute I saw her I knew she had no idea what type of club she had ventured into and that she was straight. She was pretty. She had her hair in these two-crazy big afro puffs on each side of her head. Her earrings were huge wooden pieces with Africa painted on them. She wore jeans that looked painted on and a tight fitted knit top that stopped short at her waist. Where that top stopped was like an arrow pointing to her ass saying "Look at me." And she had plenty of ass to look at. I knew that it wasn't going to take long before another stud approached her and probably scared her to death. I walked over to her table and sat down.

      "Hello, my name is Lee." I introduced myself. She looked up and paused for a minute. I laughed because I knew she was trying to figure out if I was a girl, a boy, or some type of hybrid combination of both.

      "I'm sorry." She says after she realized that she had been staring at me without introducing herself.

      "My name is Rayne. Nice to meet you, Lee." She extended her hand and I reach out to shake it.

      "So Miss Rayne, how often do you come to a place like this?" I questioned her.

      "This is the first time I've been to a club. I was married, well I am married, but I'm not with my husband because he cheated, he cheated a lot and I got tired of it so after the last time I caught him I said enough is enough and I wasn't going to sit around and wait on him anymore so I decided to come out and see if I could meet someone although I've never dated before. I mean other than my husband and my first boyfriend, Trent." She rambles with no pause, not even to take a breath.

"Ok, I wasn't expecting all that but you obviously needed to get that off your chest," I laugh.

      She smiles and blushes, "I'm sorry, I don't know you and I'm telling you all my problems. I just thought I would come out and see if I could find a nice man but I don't see many here tonight." She scans the bar.

"There are plenty of men here except most of them are in dresses. You aren't going to find many straight men in here." I tell her.

"What do you mean?" She asked with a puzzled look.

"You are in a gay bar." I informed her.

"Shut the front door. Am I really? I didn't even notice." She says looking around the club.

"Mum the club is called the Rainbow Room and there are Rainbows everywhere you look." I am amused.

"I just thought it looked like a happy place." She laughs and continues, "Gay means Happy." She laughs again.

"Rainbows are a gay pride thing. I always assume everyone knows that."

"Well, I didn't. I've never been around any gay people."

"I'm sure you have; gay people are everywhere. You probably wouldn't notice them unless someone was holding up a sign saying, "I'm queer and I'm here." I laughed.

"Why do you think it's so funny that I just made a mistake? Don't laugh at me." She says incensed. "Who are you to pass judgement on me? I'll leave you and your little gay bar to all the gays." She stands up to storm out but knocks my drink over.

"I'm sorry. I didn't mean to, here let me get some napkins." Her face is red and she is obviously flustered.

"It's ok and look I'm sorry. I wasn't making fun of you."

"Yes, you were."

"Ok, maybe a little bit." I smile and Rayne returns with a smile of her own.

"Come on, I'll walk you out to your car." I offered.

"Ok." She said
and we head to the door.

When we get outside, Rayne starts laughing.

"What's so funny?" I asked.

"I guess I can scratch going to a gay club off my bucket list."

"Oh, if going to a gay club is on there, I would like to see what else you got on that bucket list."

By the time we get to Rayne's car she has stopped laughing and has a serious look on her face. I can see the wheels in her head churning.

"Is there something wrong?"

"It's just that I don't want to go back home. I'm just not ready to face him."

"There's an IHOP around the corner if you want to go have some coffee, get a bite to eat or something. People say I'm a great listener, if you just need an ear."

"I would love that."

We leave our cars parked and walk the couple of blocks to IHOP. The hostess takes us to a booth in the corner and we take a seat. Our waitress brings us our menu and leaves us to make our decisions.

"Are you hungry?" I asked.

"Starving!" Rayne replies.

"Good, because I didn't want to order a bunch of food and smash it in front of you while you were sipping on a cup of coffee."

Our waitress returned and Rayne ordered a chicken fajita omelet and hash browns. I get a T-bone steak, eggs over easy and hash browns. We both have pancakes with strawberries and whip cream.

"Can I ask you a question?"

"Sure, Miss Rayne, you can ask me anything?"

"What exactly do you classify yourself as? I mean I can see that you are an attractive woman but you dress like a man, act like a man, walk and talk like a man, so I was just curious as to what you label yourself?"

"There are a bunch of categories and subcategories when it comes to the LGBT community. I am bisexual because I am still attracted to men. By appearance an action most would refer to me as a soft stud because I have masculine qualities but I'm still an attractive semi-feminine woman. I can transition easily from being stud to femme."

"Stud? Femme? I don't know what all that means."

"I could give you a tutorial if you like."

"Well, I have nothing but time, you know I'm trying to avoid going home. So please enlighten me Obie Wan Kenobi" She says with an exaggerated bow of her head and her hands are in the prayer position.

"Ok where here it goes. Now mind you the list I am about to give you is not all inclusive because there are always those that may fall somewhere in between two categories or may be in a whole different category altogether."

"I got you just give me the condensed version." Rayne sat up and looked at me intensely. She was curious about the girl-on-girl thing.

"Ok, most lesbians are classified as either stud or femme. There are various subcategories between the two."

"Wait." Rayne stops me. "What's a stud and what's a femme?"

"Studs are the girls that look more like boys. Femmes are the girls that look like, well, like girls."

"Oh ok. I got it now. You can continue." She says.

I began to go through the list of subcategories.
"The true stud is a little confusing. She thinks like a man and acts like a man. She takes on the very dominant male role in a relationship. She always dresses like a man down to her boxer shorts. There is nothing girly about her. She is sometimes more of a man than some men. In bed, she will only make love to her women with a strap on.

A New Age Stud is the tomboy that everybody knew growing up; the girl that would rather play basketball with the boys than jump rope with the girls. She may use a strap on in the bed from time to time but it is not necessary.

The Fem-Stud is a lesbian that is all girl but has stud like qualities. She is so fly that men are attracted to her, even though she is obviously gay. She is usually dominating in the bedroom.

The Pseudo stud is a pretender. She is not a true stud but only acts like a stud in front of her stud friends.

Fake Studs are femmes that act like True Studs to attract another femme. She will try to assume the dominant stud role, but she is living a lie. I call this the old bait-and-switch lesbian.

Lastly just like gay men can be versatile, a top or a bottom, some lesbians are also versatile. She can be attracted to a stud or a femme. She likes what is pleasing to her eyes. If she is with a stud, she acts the submissive part and is totally femme. When she is with a femme, she plays the dominant stud role."

I pause for a minute to let everything sink in.

"Are you following me so far? Am I going too fast?" I ask.

"You're doing a great job. Keep going, I'm all ears." Rayne replies.

"Ok, FEMMES are the girly types and they can be…"
A Pillow Princess, this is the type that usually gets with a True Stud. She doesn't eat pussy because she never had to or doesn't want to. She treats her stud just like a woman would treat her man.
A New Age femme is all woman but she enjoys eating pussy so will probably not date a True Stud. She will, however, mess around with other femmes.
A Dominant/Aggressive femme loves being the dominant one in the bedroom. Sometimes she will take on a fake stud role to attract femmes since that is her preference. Even though she is femme, she may experiment with a strap on, just to enhance her dominance over her partner."

"So Femmes are the ones that look like normal women?" Rayne asks.

"All lesbians are normal women."

"I'm sorry." Rayne apologizes.

"It's ok." I respond back before continuing.

"BISEXUAL WOMEN are classified as…
True Bisexuals because like the pendulum on a clock, they swing back and forth. Even though they are attracted to both they can have loving, meaningful relationships with either. When she is with a woman, she is with her, and fits totally into the gay world with no problems. When she is with a man, she fits totally into the straight world. I would put myself into this category.
Fake bi-sexual/Tri-sexual Women are the type of women that are not bisexual. She is just having sex with a woman for the "freak factor." In other words, she is just freaky in bed, and that is all it is to her "just being freaky." She will usually have a boyfriend and want him to join in on the fun. They are mostly only attracted to femme women, because this is the only type of woman that their man will allow in the bedroom.
CURIOUS FEMALES are usually fascinated by the gay community but have reservations. They will usually start out being bisexual, but closeted until they decide to go one way or the other.

SIKE-A-DYKES are the women who claim to be 100% lesbian, but they still mess with men on the low. One week they could be gay and the next they could be pregnant.

Bullshit Studs do not represent studs well at all. They are usually looking for a femme to take care of them. In other words, they are the equivalent of a good for nothing scrub of a man.

You have women that are Polyamorous, which means they can have loving committed relationships with multiple people. Those people may or may not have a relationship with each other. Then there are those that are Pansexual. They are sexually attracted to a person despite their gender or sexual identity. This woman could love transgender, gay men, lesbians, heterosexuals and so on."

I finish my lesson.

Rayne listened intently to my class, Lesbianism 101. Sometimes she looked like she wanted to ask questions but she let me keep talking.

"You look even more confused. What is it?" I ask.

"So you have sex with men and women?"

"Yes" I reply.

"But you dress in men's clothes?"

"Not all the time. I'm versatile. I can fit into the lesbian community as a stud or I can fit in the straight community, trust me when it's time to be feminine, I clean up pretty nicely."

"Do you wear a strap-on?" She asks.

"Sometimes." I answer back

"Do you prefer femmes or studs?"

"I only date femmes. I am too dominating to ever date a stud. I am into the pretty girls like you."

Rayne blushes and looks down at her plate.

"Have you ever thought about what it would be like to be with a woman?" I ask her.

"No, I'm not gay so why would I ever think about being with a woman." Rayne looked annoyed.

"Don't knock it until you try it.

"We can't just go around trying stuff all willy nilly."

"I think you should try most things at least once in your life."

"I'll pass."

"Ok, but this is a standing offer. You ready to get out of here?"

"Yes and thank you for buying me dinner, or breakfast. Not really sure what to call it."

"No problem."

I leave a tip on the table and go to the register to pay the check. Rayne and I head back the few blocks to her car. She unlocks her door and I open it for her. She thanks me again for keeping her company.

"You know if you had gone to dinner with a man and he was a perfect gentleman and a great listener. You would at least give him a goodbye kiss."

"Yeah, but you are not a man."

"Well, we can pretend tonight. If you had going to a gay club on your bucket list, I'm sure kissing a girl must be on there somewhere. Ask Katy Perry, she kissed a girl and liked it." I laughed and so does Rayne. I noticed she only had one dimple on her left cheek. This girl was cute and honestly straight or not, I was feeling her.

"So do I get a kiss or what?" I persist.

"Ok, I might as well strike that off my bucket list too." She finally relents.

I step close to her and press my body against hers. She leaned back against the car and I looked her in her eyes. Poor little Rayne, she has no clue that the art of seduction is what I get off on. This kiss is only going to be the first step, I'm going to have all of her, and she just doesn't know it yet.

"I don't go straight in for a kiss on the lips, is that ok?"

"Yes, that's fine."

I kiss her on the cheek first and slide my kiss just a little so that my lips are on her ear. I kiss her ear and I feel her shiver a little. I know she likes it. I move back to her cheek and then to her lips. I kiss her softly at first, sweetly. I feel her relax and I part her lips with my tongue. I take her bottom lip between mine and give it a little suck before I go back to kissing her. She begins to moan while we are kissing. "Yes, I got her." I think to myself. She is enjoying this so now it's time to stop. The first step to seduction is always leave them wanting more.

I pull away and open her car door again. I scribble my number on a piece of paper and give it to her. When she sits in the car, I lean in and grab her seat belt. My body rubs against her breast as I fastened her seatbelt for her.

"Text me and let me know you made it home safely. If you don't I'm going to be worried about you."

"Ok, I will."

"You promise?" I asked.

"I promise." She swears holding up her hand and crossing her heart.

"Ok baby, be safe and I'll be waiting on your text."

Rayne gets in her car and drives away. When she texts me then I'll have her number and the games can begin.

Rayne

My mind wouldn't slow down on the drive home. I had so many thoughts going on, like I had just kissed a girl. Oh my God!!! I have never done anything like that. I had never thought about doing anything like that so it was strange that I was so excited by it.

When it came to kissing, I didn't think it could get better than Quest but Lee gave me probably the best kiss of my life. When her lips touched mine, I felt Miss Millie (my pet name for my pussy) come to life. Oh, honey, she got to throbbing and I had to tell her to settle down. There will be none of that because Lee is a girl and I am straight. But if I was straight would Miss Millie have reacted to her the way she did? If I was straight, then I should not have liked it, right? Damn I am confused as hell. I couldn't stop thinking about the way her body felt when she pressed it against mine. I could feel her breast against my breast and it felt good. I wanted to grab her and pull her against me. I thought about grabbing her ass. Shit, what am I doing? Maybe it's just because I'm still hurt over what Quest did. You know this could just be me acting out like a child does to be rebellious against a parent's rule. I was straight. I knew I was straight. I loved men. I loved everything about men. The way they looked, smelled, felt, and tasted. I could never get that from a woman so I don't understand why a woman would choose another woman over a man. Even if she was a pseudo-man like Lee. It's just unnatural for two women to be together. It was wrong, even the Bible said it was wrong. Hell, maybe that is why it felt so good.

Well it wasn't like I was going to ever see Lee again. So, I don't have to worry about any of this stuff. I pull into the driveway and I'm grateful that I don't see Quest's car. If he was home, then I was going to go spend the night at a hotel. First thing in the morning I am getting all the locks changed and changing the password on the security system.

Once I got in the house, I kicked off my shoes because my feet were killing me. I pulled my phone out of my purse to put it on the charger and that is when I see Lee's number on the piece of paper she gave me. I did promise her that I would text and let her know I made it home safely. It was nice that she cared. I sent her a simple text… *This is Rayne, I'm home. Thanks again.*

I headed to the bathroom so I could shower and get ready for bed. This has been a long night and I am exhausted. I go to the bathroom, get undressed and jump in the shower. The hot water feels so good and I am feeling relaxed but Lee pops up in my mind. Damnit, I thought I had put those thoughts to bed. Why couldn't I stop thinking about her? Ms. Millie woke up when I thought of Lee. I'm looking down at her and thinking this bitch better go back to sleep because there will be none of that dyke shit going on between me and Lee.

"I am a girl, Ms. Millie, in case you didn't get the memo and girls don't fuck other girls." I'm having a dialogue with my vagina in the shower. I remove the hand-held shower and spray water against my pussy which made Miss Millie wake up even more. Ok, fine. I may not have a man to take care of her but I still had a box of toys beside my bed. I dry off, get in bed and reach into my toy box. It looks like it's going to be a match between Ms. Millie and my silver bullet. Before I could get start, I hear the key turn in the door. Damn, I forgot we kept a spare key hidden outside just in case we accidentally got locked out. I put my bullet under my pillow and pretend to be asleep. Quest got in bed behind me and wrapped his arms around me.

"I'm so sorry. Baby you know I love you. I think I have a problem. Maybe we can go to counseling or something. I really want us to work."

He begins to nibble on my ear and very slowly runs his erect dick across my ass. He gently rocks back and forth and I'm lost in the pleasure, in the moment. I savor the touch of his skin against mine. I turn over to face him. I kiss him and my kisses sink soothingly into his mouth, sending pleasure chills throughout my body. I love this man with every fiber of my being. Sometimes I craved him more than my next breath. I have loved him in all the way that I should have and in all the ways that matter and I knew I couldn't just stop loving him now.

By the next morning all was forgiven. I am in his arms with my cheek pressed against his chest. I looked up into his eyes and he bends down to kiss me on the forehead. I melted. I just wanted to lie like this with him holding me forever.

Quest

I knew how lucky I was to have Rayne forgive me. I didn't deserve it but she did it and I was determined to do right this time. No more fucking around for me, period. When I told Rayne that my cheating days were over she looked at me like I had lost my mind. But I don't care, I'm going to prove it to her. This morning I am going to cook breakfast for her. It's been a long time since I have cooked for her even though I am a good cook. My mom made sure all her sons knew how to cook and clean. I used my cooking skills to pick up girls when I was in college.

The pots and pans rattled even though I moved slowly trying to be as quiet as possible. I cooked some bacon, eggs and made pancakes. She loved pancakes with strawberries and whipped cream. I poured a tall glass of orange juice and put her food on a serving tray.

When I walked into the bedroom Rayne was still. She had fallen back to sleep. I kissed her until she woke up. She is grumpy when she is awakened from her sleep. She swings her hand at me to shoo me away.

"Baby, I have your breakfast. Wake up and eat while it is still hot."

She rolls over and stretches.

"Good Morning." She says groggily.

She gets up and goes to the bathroom and when she returns she props herself up on a stack of pillows and I put her tray on her lap.

"I feel really special. It's been forever since you cooked me breakfast and you haven't brought me breakfast in bed since we first got married."

"I am a reformed man." Quest looked serious. "Rayne, I promise, you are going to see a new man in me. I am going to be the best husband you could ever have. I promise I am going to spend the rest of my life making you happy."

I could tell by the faces that she was making, Rayne was skeptical. Her lips were turned up at the corner and she looked at me side eyed. Actions speak louder than words. I am going to show her the new Quest. I'm going to prove it to her. All I need is a little time and for her to be patient. Hopefully, in time, she will move on to the next chapter of our life and we don't have to keep re-reading the last one.

Lee

I was glad to get a text from Rayne. She let me know she had made it home safely. It probably would have scared her if I came straight out and asked her for her phone number. That would have seemed too much like a dude trying to make a move on her.

I decided after a few days I would give her a call just to check in on her and make sure she was ok. I dialed her number and waited on her to pick up.

"Hello."

"Hello Rayne, this is Lee."

"Oh, Hi Lee. I wasn't expecting you to call me."

"I know you weren't but I was just thinking about what you told me about your husband and all and I just wanted to make sure you were ok."

"Yes, we are fine. We made up, so everything is all good."

"That's great." I say out loud but I'm cursing on the inside.

"Well, you should let me take you out again to celebrate or you should return the favor and take me out to eat."

"I don't know about that." Rayne said reluctantly.

"It's just a friendly date. We can forget about that little experimental kiss. Even though I think you are sexy, I just want to be your friend and honestly, you look like you could use a good friend."

There was a long pause on the other end of the phone.

"What do you have in mind?" Rayne finally asked.

"I'm open to whatever you want to do. You make the call and I'll follow your lead."

"I'm ok with visiting the club again. At least this time I will know what type of club it is and maybe I can enjoy the experience."

"Ok, that sounds good. We can meet there around 9 if that is good with you."

"Sounds good to me. I will meet you there."

"You are not going to stand me up, are you?"

"No, I'm looking forward to seeing you again. You have really educated me and I would like to learn more."

"Ok, I'm an open book so get your questions ready and I'll answer them as best as I can."

"I sure will. I guess I'll see you tonight."

"I hope so because I'll be waiting"

I hung up the phone. I have to make sure that my outfit is on fleek. I step into my closet to pick out my look for tonight. When she met me I was wearing some baggy jeans and a short sleeve collar shirt. I had on some timberland boots and my hair was braided to the back.

I thought I would give her a different look tonight. I selected a black Armani suit. It was a timeless style that was elegant and sophisticated. I brushed my hair back into a ponytail and let it hang freely down my back. Yes, this time she would get to see another side of me, the debonair Lee.

Women don't intimidate me but the closer it gets to my date with Rayne the more nervous I become. I am very good at the art of seduction even when it comes to women who think they are straight. I always tell people at least 95% of all women fall somewhere between bi-curious and lesbian. Sex with a woman came easy for me, what managed to elude me were the real feelings. Women were just for fun, for pleasure. I have never been in love with a woman but I have been in love with man before. From the first night, I met Rayne, I couldn't stop thinking about her. It wasn't that I wanted to sleep with her. It was more than that. She wasn't the typical woman. She was different, special and that is why she had my attention. Tonight, I was going to show her another side of me, my soft romantic side.

I get to the club much earlier than the time I told Rayne to meet me. The owner of the club is, Giselle, a transgender woman that most of us considered our mother. She was beautiful, confident and unapologetically honest. Every night at the club she was dressed like she was going to some red-carpet event. She was super feminine and had a walk that any runway model would envy.

"Darling, I got you the hook-up. Whoever your friend is must be really special because you have never asked Mother for anything like this before." Giselle says, talking even more with her hands then her mouth.

"I really appreciate you doing this for me. I owe you one." I say gratefully.

"Child, you know Mother would do anything for one of her children. I don't expect anything from you. You are one of the good ones, not like some of my other problem children. I have always been the proudest of you." Giselle stops long enough to wrap her arms around me and give me a squeeze.

"Thanks Mother, you know I love you."

We reach one of the VIP rooms in the back of the club and Giselle pauses before opening the door with a flourish. She had outdone herself with this one. The room was beautifully draped with white satin fabric. There was a small white bistro table with two chairs and a beautiful arrangement of various white flowers. There was a long white sofa against one wall and a small buffet table against the other wall. There was a bottle of champagne on ice and a tray of various cheeses, fruits and decadent chocolates. The room was sound proof and had its own music with a remote control that could adjust the sound and the lighting. Everything was perfect.

I went back into the club and waited on Rayne to show up. It was 9:30 now and she wasn't here yet. I was starting to get nervous and was thinking she had stood me up when I got a text from her. She was outside. I walk outside to meet her and she looks amazing. I lead her into the club and we head toward the dance floor.
Rayne stops and pulls back on my arm.

"What's wrong?"

"I can't dance."

I laugh. "We aren't going to the dance floor. We are going past the dance floor. Don't worry."

"Ok." She sighs with relief and loosens her grip on my arm.

I take her to the VIP room that Giselle has prepared for us and open the door to allow Rayne to walk in first. She stands in the doorway with her mouth open looking around at everything.

"This is beautiful." She finally speaks.

"Thank you. Would you like to sit on the couch or at the table?"

"The sofa will be fine, thank you." She replies.

I take her by the hand and walk her to the sofa.

"You did all this for me?" Rayne is still looking around the room.

"Well, technically the club owner, Giselle, did it. I just made the request."

"You must have some pull with her."

"Giselle and I go way back."

"Is she one of your girlfriends?"

"Ok, first why did you say, one of, like I have a bunch of women and secondly no, she is not. We are friends. She is more like a mother to me." I reply.

"I'm sorry." Rayne apologizes. "I am making assumptions. If you were a guy and did all these things, I would think you were a player trying to get into my panties."

"So now you think I'm not trying to get in your panties?" I smile.

Rayne laughs, "So are you admitting that this is about getting me into your bed."

"Why would I have to get you into my bed when we have a perfectly good couch right here?" I pat the empty seat cushion beside me.

"You are a mess; you know that right?"

"I've been called worse, so thank you."

Rayne laughs again. Her mood is light and she is more comfortable with me then the first time we met. We enjoy champagne and I put on some soft music while we talk and get to know each other. Rayne is talking but I am staring at her lips. She had the sexiest heart shaped lips on the planet. I wanted to kiss her so bad but I don't want to scare her by being too aggressive.

Rayne

My hands will not stop shaking and I don't know if it is from fear or excitement. I am afraid of the unknown but excited about the possibilities. Lee had invited me to her house and I readily agreed. I followed her and when she pulled into the driveway; I pulled in beside her. She walks to my car and opens my door. She grabs my hand and leads me into the house. Her house is beautifully decorated. She leaves me sitting on the couch while she disappears into the bedroom. In a few minutes, she comes back to get me.

"First, you have to make me a promise." Lee said.

"Anything." I reply.

"Promise me that you will not fight me. Promise me that you will just allow whatever is going to happen to happen. Can you promise me that?"

"Yes."

She takes my hand and leads me to the bedroom. In the middle of the floor there was a huge freestanding bed. She leads me past the bed into the bathroom. The candlelit bathroom smelled like jasmine. All around the tub were beautiful white candles and tulips; tulips not roses. Just the sight of those flowers was enough to make my pussy throb. The Jacuzzi tub was ready.

She stopped me in front of the tub and looked me in my eyes. My knees buckled. I tried to speak but words would not form.

She puts her finger to my lips.

"Don't speak."

I am silenced.

"I am going to show you how a woman should be made love to."

"Yes, Please." I wanted to say but I remained quiet.

She removed my glasses and placed them on the white marble counter. She started taking the hair pins out of my hair. My natural hair is big and unruly so I normally braid it and pin it. Damn, I wish I had flat ironed my hair because now my hair is this big poof and I'm sure this Angela Davis afro is not sexy at all. I'm lost in my thoughts until I feel my head snap back. She grabbed a handful of my hair and pulled it back until my neck is completely exposed. She kisses me on my neck and I shudder.

"I love your hair like this." She says, almost as if she had read my mind and knew my doubt.

She pulls my hair harder while she kisses and licks the entire length of my neck. I am so hot and my legs are shaking. I'm holding on to her arms to steady myself. She stops.

"Raise your arms."

I obey and with one swift move my top is on the floor. Her tongue traces down the crease of my cleavage while her hands run up my back. I didn't feel her unsnap my bra but I felt it coming off. This girl was good. She stepped back long enough to allow my bra to slide down my arms and join my top on the floor. My breast hangs freely, exposed to her, ready for her.

My nipples are hard with anticipation and she doesn't disappoint them. She takes one in her mouth and starts to suck while her hand caresses the other one. Her free hand has found the button on my jeans. Within minutes my jeans and underwear have joined the rest of my clothes. I am fully naked. Lee continues the assault on my nipples, her tongue making soft circles around one then the other. She slid her hand down to my pussy and I am thinking if she just barely touches my clit I am going to cum. I brace myself for the explosion but she stops. Her hands go back around my waist and she pulls me in close. We kiss some more and it's amazing. My heart is beating fast and I can't catch my breath. She pulls my lower lip into her mouth and sucks. I don't know what it is about her sucking on my lips but it feels like there is a string going from my lips to my pussy and every time she sucks my lips, my pussy pulsates with pleasure. Damn, I feel like I am going to cum just from kissing. I'm trying to talk myself down from this high that I am on.

She stops again before I can climax.

"Don't stop." I beg.

"SSSSHHHHHH." She puts her finger against my lips to silence my pleas and I immediately obey. I stand before her silently waiting for whatever pleasure she has planned for me.

"Close your eyes."

Without question, I close my eyes.

"Good, I love it when you are submissive."

The soft fabric brushes against my forehead before covering my eyes. She was blindfolding me. My excitement elevated. She grabbed my hand and led me up the stairs and then back down into the sunken tub. She placed a pillow behind my head and instructed me to lie my head back. I sink down in the tub enjoying the heat and the weightlessness of my body in the water. Music had been playing the whole time but my ears had tuned it out as background noise until now. I can't believe she is playing *Adore* by Prince. *Adore* is one of my favorite songs of all time. How does she know what I like? The sponge rubs down my left arm first. She was bathing me. Every stroke across my body is more sensual then the next. When she is done, she orders me to stand and I comply. With the blindfold, still in place, I stand in front of her while she rubs a towel up and down each arm then each thigh. The towel continues up my thigh until it reaches my pussy. She gives the towel a little twirl to dry her off a little before she turns me around to finish drying me. I turn around so that my back is to her and she starts drying at my shoulders and slowly moves down to my back. When she reached my ass, she lingers there making soft circles with the towel. Even this simple act is foreplay to me. She grabs my hand and leads me to the bed.

"Lie down on your stomach."
I obey. She straddles my lower back. She is naked. As she begins to massage my shoulder her body is gliding up and down from the small of my back to the top of my ass. I can feel her clit against my skin. I am so aroused, I move with her, back and forth grinding my pussy against the firm mattress.

"I did not tell you to move." She speaks with such authority that I stop immediately.

"That's a good girl." She whispers in my ear before asking me to turn over.

"Sit up." I do exactly what I'm told.

"Open your mouth." I obey

I sit on the edge of the bed with my mouth opened, anxiously awaiting what she was going to give me.
I recognized the taste of strawberries and cream when it touches my tongue. She feeds me strawberries and in between each strawberry, she kisses me. Next, I feel a glass touch my lips as she offers me a drink. I take a sip. It is champagne.

"You are being such a good girl. It makes me happy when you submit to me this way." She whispered in my ear.

Her finger is pressed against my lips just like the strawberry had been before it. I take it into my mouth and began to suck. She rubs her finger in and out against my tongue. Just sucking her finger had me hotter than a firecracker. I wanted more. I wanted to run my tongue between each finger, wanted my mouth filled. I tried to put another finger in my mouth but she snatches her hand away.

"Why are you trying to take more than what I offer you?" I stop immediately. She was displeased with my actions.

"I'm sorry." I respond.

"Did I tell you to speak?" She questioned.

I fell silent again.

"Do I make you feel good?" I nod my head in agreement.

"Do you want me to stop pleasuring you?" She asked.

I wanted to shout, "hell no, I don't want you to stop, EVER!" But I know better so I just shake my head.

"You disobeyed me, you will be punished."

She told me to open my mouth again and she gave me her finger. This time I was happy to just suck on her one finger without being greedy for more.

"Open your legs." I oblige.

She withdrew her finger from my mouth and starts fingering me with that same finger. A dick would not have felt any better to me than Lee's finger. Within a few minutes I feel my orgasm building, I am about to cum. I thought, please, please, don't stop. This time she doesn't and I cum in massive convulsions. I lose all control. She withdraws her hand, leaving me shaking and moaning on the edge of the bed.

"Since you disobeyed me this is all the pleasure I will give you tonight. I had more planned but you must be punished. Now get dressed and go home."

I pull the blindfold down and open my eyes to see if she was serious. She was. I can't believe she is going to finger fuck me and send me home like this. No kiss; no hug; nothing. As I get dressed, Lee disappears into the back of the house. I waited around but she never returned. When I find her she is in her office on the phone. She just looked up and waved good-bye in a dismissive way. I backed out of her office door and left. In the car, I replay what just happened over in my mind. Even though my feelings were hurt, I had to admit this girl excited me. If she wanted to be the teacher I was ready to be the eager student. Next time I'll be sure to follow all instructions.

I had given up so much to Quest without a fight, without a request, just a fearful surrender. Now here I am willingly submitting my control to a woman. In a strange way, I was not afraid, or fearful. I felt empowered. Even though I may receive "punishment" it is my choice to follow or refuse. Submission is a gift but am I ready to let go? To find out how far I am willing to go with my permission? Did I want to know how adventurous I could be or how restrained?

Baylor

I was in one of those moods so I was anxious for my wife to get home. Alicia walked through the door looking as beautiful as the day I met her. Even though I know my opinion is a little bias, I think I have the best wife on the planet.

I never met anyone as open and as honest as she was. She understood me so well. Maybe some of it was because she was a therapist but I believe a lot of it has to do with her strong personality.

When I met Alicia, I was a college student going through an identity crisis. I had left my family behind and never looked back. Because my Uncle had molested me for so many years it made me question my sexuality. In college, I started experimenting with men even though I was attracted to women. I enjoyed the sex with other men but I always felt like shit after. I would be sick to my stomach the minute it was over with but I didn't stop. I was so confused and screwed up that I wanted to die.

Alicia saved me. I had left out of the dorm room of one of the men that I was having sex with on campus and as I was walking back to my place, I literally bumped into her. I was trying to apologize to her but she was concerned about what was causing my tears.

"What's wrong?" She asked genuinely concerned.

Her question would have normally elicited an automatic answer. I always put a smile on my face and said that I was fine. I was great. Everything was all good. I had learned to show the world a happy face even though I was dying inside. I was tired of living a lie.

She invited me back to her room and even though she was a stranger I felt comfortable with her immediately. Her voice was soothing and it was like truth serum to me. For the first time in my life, I told the entire truth. I told her everything about my childhood, my mother abandoning me, my uncle molesting me, my suicidal thoughts and about my affairs with other men. Alicia listened intently to everything I said. When I finished, I expected her to freak out, to judge me, to tell me to get up and get the hell out of her room; but she didn't. She reached over and hugged me, tightly. I couldn't hold back my emotions or tears. All she did was hold me until I stopped crying.

"There is nothing wrong with you." She began to explain. "The reason you feel so bad after having sex with men is because you are not gay. You aren't attracted to men you just like anal play. Because your uncle abused you at a time when you were beginning to develop your sexual identity it made you confused. You don't need a man; you need a woman that understands a man that likes anal play is not gay."

"How do you feel about a man like that?" I asked her.

"I think it is perfectly normal and it doesn't make you gay. What makes a man gay is if he is only attracted to men. You obviously are not attracted to men and that is why you feel sick afterwards. I bet that you keep your eyes closed the entire time and fantasize about a woman"

She was right. If I didn't imagine myself being with a woman, then nothing would happen. From that day on, Alicia and I became a couple. Within a few months I proposed to her and she said yes. As soon as we graduated from college we got married. My time with Alicia had been the best. She truly made me happy.

I was excited that she came home early. I was looking forward to seeing her. When she walked in, I took her briefcase from her and let her hold on to my shoulder while she took off her shoes.

"I'm so tired."

"Don't worry baby. I cooked dinner and I have your bathwater ready."

"You are the best, thank you baby."
I led her to the bathroom and helped her get undressed and into the tub. While she soaked in the tub I brought her a glass of wine.

"I'm going to finish up dinner so when you get ready just come to the kitchen.

I go back to the kitchen and checked on the garlic parmesan chicken that I had in the oven. It was ready so I turn the oven down low just to keep it warm until we were ready to eat. I made a Greek salad with romaine lettuce, cucumbers, tomatoes, black olives, and Feta cheese to accompany the chicken. It was a simple and light dinner. I didn't want us to get too full because I had plans for tonight.

Alicia came into the kitchen in her bathrobe. She sat at the table and I brought her a plate of food and refilled her wine glass. While we enjoyed our dinner, she told me about her day. When we finish dinner, I loaded the dishwasher and we headed to the bedroom.

Alicia disappeared into the bathroom and when she returned she was naked. I take Alicia by the hand and lead her to the bed. She is lying on her back, I got on my knees and she puts her legs on my shoulders as I buried my face in her pussy.

I love the way her pussy taste, love the smell, love the feel of it against my tongue. She would grab my head and grind her pussy all over face. I couldn't get enough of her addictive pussy.

Normally, she is quiet and reserved but when she is about to cum she loses control. Her moans turn into screams and she thrashes around uncontrollably before she squirts wetting my face, the bed and anything else close to her. After, she takes a moment to come down from her high she orders me to lie on the bed.

Alicia takes my already hard dick into her mouth and begins to suck. She moves down to my balls licking them softly before she put one then both in her mouth. She stroked my dick while she was giving my balls special attention. Her tongue slides down to that spot between my balls and asshole, her tongue sending shivers down my spine. She then slides her tongue down to my asshole and begins to lick it. I am in heaven, having my asshole licked is such a turn on. She strokes my dick the entire time her tongue is licking my ass. She comes back up and starts sucking my dick again. She loved giving head and my moans just propelled her to suck longer and deeper. She replaced her tongue with a finger in my ass and the feeling of her sucking my dick and fingering my asshole is more than I can take. I cum in her mouth and she swallows it all.

"Turn over." She instructed.

I follow her command. I hear her open the drawer to the nightstand and I already know what she is doing. She is getting her strap-on out so that we can play. Alicia loved that I allowed her to be dominant in the bedroom. She loved our role play and we both loved that we could do whatever we wanted sexually without inhibitions or judgement. She takes some lubricant out and lubes her strap on before taking a lubricated finger and sticking it in my ass. Alicia is the one that taught me about "prostate milking". She stuck a finger in my ass and moved it back and forth against my prostate like her finger was telling it to come here. Without an erection or any stimulation to my dick, I nutted. She was amazing.

She gets positioned behind me and I feel the tip of her strap enter my ass. She introduced a little bit of her strap at a time allowing my ass to adjust to the size. I relax my muscles and she can insert the entire length of the dildo in my ass. It feels incredible having her fuck my ass. She is fucking me and even though my dick isn't hard I still orgasm. It only takes a few minutes for her to get me back up and I fuck her until we both climax again and fall asleep wrapped in each other's arms.

Once she and I started having sex, I never slept with another man. Alicia never made me feel bad about enjoying anal sex and she never once questioned my manhood. There were times when I thought about my past life. I thought about those men that I would sneak in back doors to see. How we would have wild, crazy sex all night and once the sun came up we would pass each other in the streets like we were total strangers. I didn't miss those days. I was happy and fulfilled with my wife. We were soulmates.

Rayne

I got a phone call from Lee today. She wanted to see me again. My punishment was over and she had promised to show me another level of pleasure today. I take a shower and get ready to go to her house. The entire ride to Lee's house, I am thinking about our first time together; so, by the time I arrived at her house my panties are soaked. When I get there, I found a note on the front door.

You know where the key is.
Let yourself in, get naked and wait for me in bed.
I'll be there shortly.
Lee

Anticipation made my pussy throb. I was so excited that I dropped the key before picking it up and finally letting myself in the house. I did as I was instructed and went to the bedroom. I got completely naked and arranged myself on the bed and waited on her.

I waited so long that I dozed off. I am startled awake by a gentle kiss on the forehead. Lee is butt naked. Oh my God!!! I feel like I am still dreaming. Her body is beautiful, not that anyone could tell. She never wore clothes that showed her figure and no one would guess underneath those clothes was a shape that video vixens would die for. She is freshly washed, beautifully scented, and has a demure air about her that was even harder to believe than her body. At this moment, she was not my master; she was my mistress. Dear God, is this what Quest feels like when he is about to have sex with a different woman?

"Have you missed me?" Lee asked.

"More than you can imagine."

"Did you think about me?"

"All the time."

"Good, are you ready?"

"Yesssssss!" I shouted.

"You are a little too anxious." Lee laughed.

"We are going to take it slow. I know all of this is new for you and I don't want to overwhelm you. So, we will take it slow. You will enjoy each new experience and I will continue to give you pleasure if you never disobey or question me. Do you understand?" I nod.

Lee got in bed and I felt her body press against the full length of mine. She was so soft and the feel of her skin against mine was exquisite. At the same time, it was weird to touch her. I had never touched another woman's breast before. Lee grabbed my hand and cupped my hand around her breasts. Damn, no wonder men were so fascinated with boobies. She began to kiss and suck on my nipples while I played with hers. She took her hand off my breast long enough to slide it down to my already wet pussy. I spread my legs, needing to feel her touch me again. She stuck her finger in my pussy just long enough to get it wet before she started to rub my clit.

"Lee, baby, you make me feel so good." I whisper in her ear. She immediately pulled away.

"I've already pleasured you with my fingers. I can't do that again. How should I pleasure you this time?"

"Will you eat my pussy? I begged.

"No, you are not ready for that yet." She replied. She must have noticed the look on my face.

"I know you have probably had your pussy eaten before but I guarantee you have never had it eaten properly. Just like I bet you have never been fucked properly. I plan to change all of that eventually. But right now, you have to take baby steps."

I didn't understand what she was trying to tell me but I wasn't going to question her or protest what she was saying. I had been with my husband for over 10 years and I can count on one hand the number of times we fucked and I didn't cum. I had an orgasm every time he ate my pussy so Lee was tripping. But I wasn't about to start an argument right now; not while my pussy was screaming for release.

"Today I am going to teach you how to grind." Lee said. I wanted to ask questions because I had no idea what grinding was but I didn't ask. I trusted Lee. If she could give me that much pleasure from a finger, I knew whatever else she had planned would be mind blowing.

She got on top of me as I lie on the bed spread eagle. She straddled me sideways where our bodies made sort of an X, like chromosomes splitting. She did a little maneuvering and that is when I felt it. Her clit was directly against my clit. I could feel her heat, her wetness. I could feel her pussy throbbing and pulsating as it came in contact and my pussy responded in unison. Lee began to rock her hips gliding her pussy back and forth across mine.

"Ohhh shit." I couldn't stop the profanity from flowing from my lips.

"What the fuck are you doing to my pussy?"

"I thought I was making it mine." Lee said

"Hell yes, you are baby. This pussy is yours. Damn, your pussy is so wet and it feels so good against me."

Lee begins to move more vigorously and her rhythm quickened as she glides against me. I grabbed her hips and wrapped my legs around her so that I could thrust up and meet her mid-stroke.

The pleasure was almost unbearable as wave after wave of orgasmic bliss swept through my body. It wasn't my first orgasm but by far this was the best I'd ever had. I felt like Neo after Morpheus gave him the red pill. My mind is awake. My eyes are wide open. My body is being pushed beyond boundaries. Again, and again I climax until I couldn't take anymore and I breathlessly begged for mercy.

"Please, I can't, please Lee, I…" I pleaded with her, unable to complete an entire sentence. That is when I found out just how deep the rabbit hole goes.

"Just breathe, baby," Lee replied. When you feel the next orgasm come on I want you to hold your breath.

Lee begins to move again. Gliding her pussy against mine and it doesn't take long for the pleasure to start building again. I was about to cum so I took a deep breath and I felt Lee's hand around my throat. She was choking me. It only lasted about 5 seconds but the orgasm was mind blowing. It became a sublime act of the spirit like an out of body experience. Lee pulled me on top of her. Wrapped her arms around me and holds me close and whispering in my ear.

"It's ok, just breathe," She repeated over and over as my body continued to shake and the tears began to fall. I wanted to talk. I wanted to tell her how I felt but I couldn't. I just held her tight until I fell asleep.

The sun coming through the cracks in the wooden plantation blinds wake me from my dreams. Where was I? I blinked a few times, trying to get my surroundings to come into focus. I sat up in the bed and looked around. She was still sleeping beside me.

"Lee." I whispered to myself before stretching back out beside her. She immediately wrapped an arm around my waist and pulled me in close. I knew the minute I walked through the door at home the questions would start. I knew I would have a hard time answering them but I didn't care. All I cared about now was being with her and how she made me feel. I had never felt so loved, so beautiful and so completely adored before. I didn't want this feeling to end, even if it meant my marriage had to.

Corey

Even though I was young when I met Rayne, I had a huge crush on her; as soon as her family moved a few houses down from mine, Rayne and I become inseparable. We spent our weekends at the skating rink. Rayne didn't know how to skate at all and stumbled around, falling often. While others laughed at her, I skated over and helped her up. I held her by her hand and helped her stay on her feet. After we had made a couple of laps around the skating rink she became more comfortable and was ready to try to skate without my assistance. She made it halfway around the rink before she fell again. This time she twisted her ankle. I tried to help her up but at the time she was much taller than I was so it was a struggle. We finally made it off the floor and she sat in a chair. I got down and pulled off her skates. I propped her foot up and went to the concession stand and got some ice in a Ziploc bag to put on her ankle. I sat beside her and waited for her mom to come and pick us up. Her mom took her to the emergency room and she allowed me to go along. From that day on Rayne and I were like conjoined twins.

Rayne was beautiful but not conceited. She was smart but not arrogant. She had a spirit of service. She didn't care about money. She was just as happy having a peanut butter and jelly sandwich as she was having a lobster dinner. She was one of a kind.

As we went through high school, I tried to move out of the friend zone but Rayne could never see me as anything other than that. It was hard for me to date other girls in school because deep down I knew I loved Rayne. She ended up dating assholes that didn't appreciate her the way that I did. Rayne was a good girl; she was wholesome and was saving herself until she got married. I had the same idea. I would save myself until I got married because deep down I hoped to marry Rayne and we would lose our virginity to each other. I was devastated when Rayne married Quest.

Since my hope of the mutual loss of virginity with Rayne died, I didn't hold on to mine much longer after she married Quest. I started dating, Harmony Nelson. She had an identical twin sister named Melody. Harmony and Melody were the most beautiful girls in the entire school and they knew it. They turned heads everywhere they went and not just because they were identical; but because they had extremely curvaceous bodies that looked built for sin.

Harmony and Melody did everything together. They continued to dress identically and wear their hair in the exact same style even into adulthood. I would often watch them walking together each step perfectly matched the other twins. They were in tune with each other and would say the same things at the same time or finish each other's sentences.

It didn't take long for Harmony to seduce me. She obviously was far from being a virgin and she opened my world to sex. The only sex I had only experienced at this point was when I would sneak and watch the porn movies my dad kept hidden under his bed while I pleasured myself. Harmony introduced me to oral sex. She loved giving head anytime and anyplace. She would suck my dick in school under the bleachers in the gym, behind buildings, even while we were at the kitchen table doing our homework. She also taught me the joy of eating pussy. My tongue would find her wet patch and trust me, her pussy stayed wet. I was hooked with my first taste of pussy. It wasn't just the taste that had me addicted it was the way that Harmony reacted whenever my tongue touched her clit. She couldn't sit still or be quiet. We almost got caught so many times. I would lick her outer lips and clit then burying my tongue deep inside her as far as I could reach licking her insides as she swirled her pussy against my face. After two months of fucking, I declared my undying love for her.

Harmony's father left when they were still babies so her mother worked two jobs to provide for her and her sister. We always had free time to fuck as much as we wanted since her mother was never around. Almost every day I was at her house, in her bed, fucking and sucking ourselves into exhaustion. I was lying on top of her and she had her legs wrapped around. Her feet resting just below my ass. I am so caught up in the feeling that I didn't hear Melody when she came in the room. She was already naked when she got in bed next to Harmony. I am dumbfounded. I look from Melody to Harmony and back. It was weird to have two of the exact same faces looking back at me.

"It's ok." Harmony says. "We share everything."

"Turn over on your back." Harmony instructed and I followed her command.

I am on my back and rock hard big pointing north. Harmony is on one side and Melody is on the other. Both lean over and put their tongue on the tip of my dick and slide down to the base. Then one has my dick in her mouth while the other one was sucked on my balls. Then they would switch. Both came up to suck on the head together. They sandwich the head of my dick between their lips. It's like they were French kissing each other and my dick just happened to be there, right in the middle. Oh, happy day!!! Their tongues flicked across my dick and each other's tongue. Harmony grabbed Melody's tits and she is squeezing them around my dick while she continues sucking the head. This must be the most amazing feeling that anyone has ever felt.

They both come up to my chest. Each one sucking a nipple, their hands are on top of each other as they stroke my dick together simultaneously. I shoot cum all over my belly. Fuck! That was not supposed to happen but I had lost control. Embarrassed I grab a tissue from Harmony's night stand and wipe the cum off my stomach. They are both giggling and I am so embarrassed that all I want to do is get out of the room as fast as possible. I stand up to get dressed so that I could leave but the twins start kissing each other and not a sisterly kiss, a lover's kiss.

What the hell, I thought. Isn't this incest? I am disgusted and excited at the same time. I feel a stirring down below as I continued watching the twins lying side by side with their hands fingering each other's pussy. It was a mirror image and sexy as hell. Harmony and Melody continued their escapades as if I wasn't in the room. They switched positions to 69 and are going to work on each other. At that moment, I thought to myself, they look alike, sound alike, walk and talk alike, surely they must taste and feel the same. My curiosity got the best of me. Melody is on top of Harmony so I licked her from behind as she straddled Harmony's face. Fuck it, I thought to myself, if they are cool with it then I am too. I pull my pants down, put a rubber on and enter Melody. Her pussy felt just as good as her sister. While I'm fucking her, Harmony is alternating between licking Melody's pussy and my balls. Melody begins to buck wildly as she starts cumming. I am holding her hips to steady myself. Once she cums, she turns on her back and Harmony puts her mouth on Melody leaving her ass high in the air for me. I fuck Harmony until the three of us climax together.

I lie between these two-beautiful sister's trying to catch my breath and get my heart to stop beating so fast. They are curled up beside me practically purring as they continue to stroke all over my body. Harmony pulls my face down for a kiss. I can still smell her sister's pussy on her lips as we kiss.

"I love you, Corey." She says.

"I love you too, Rayne." My subconscious spoke before my mouth could. That was the last night I shared a bed with either of them.

Rayne

Lee was aggressive and I had fallen for her quick and hard. Lee and I were going on a real date tonight. Normally, we just stay at her house because it was too risky for us to go out and be seen together especially since Quest and I had patched things up. He was even insisting that we go to counseling. I told him to find a marriage counselor and make an appointment and we would go together.

Tonight, Lee and I are headed to a jazz club in Columbus. Lee said the place was laid back and to not overdress so I chose a simple brown, turquoise, and cream maxi dress. I picked my hair into a big afro and pushed the front of it flat with a headband. Simple jade jewelry completed my look.

The club was nothing more than a hole in the wall; a tiny place with tall tables, bar stools and a stage. We found an empty table close to the front of the club by the stage. The band was hot. They played the kind of music that automatically made your eyes close and your head sway, your foot tap and your fingers snap. I was so caught up in the sound of the music that I didn't even notice our waitress. Lee ordered our drinks without consulting with me. It was still strange for me to be so totally submissive and trusting that I allowed her to make decisions for me. But, I must admit, I liked it. I had no idea that Lee was testing me, in fact, she was molding me.

When our waitress returned to the table with our drinks, Lee asked her to hold up for a minute. She grabbed her by her hand and pulled her down so that she could whisper something in her ear. Whatever Lee was saying must have been funny because the waitress smiled and giggled. I immediately felt possessive and a bit jealous. The waitress came over and stood by me. She was standing too close, invading my personal space to the point that I felt a little uncomfortable. Lee spoke first.

"Baby, this is our waitress, Simone. Do you think she is attractive?"

"Yes," I said not even looking up at her because she was standing too damn close.

"Would you like to kiss Simone?" Lee asked.

"No, why would I want to do that?" I questioned looking dumbfounded.

"Let me rephrase, Baby, I would like for you to kiss Simone," Lee stated.

"Lee, I really think that is inappropriate. I don't know this young lady and she is working."

Lee turns to Simone and asked her if it is ok for me to kiss her to which she replied, "Yes."

"I am not asking you, I am telling you to give Simone a kiss. You know I don't like when you don't trust me."

"I do trust you Lee. I just don't see what kissing our waitress has to do with trust."

"I asked you to do something, you should trust me enough to do it without question."

"OK, fine, I'll kiss her," I say and turn my head toward Simone who is still hovering over me with a damn smirk on her face. She bends down like she is about to kiss me but Lee stops her before it happens.

"Thank you Simone that will be all." She tipped her a twenty-dollar bill and she practically skipped away from the table.

"What was that about? You do all that fussing about me not trusting you enough to kiss her and then when I decide to do it you send her away. What kind of games are you playing?"

"I'm not playing a game. I asked you to kiss her and you should have done it without question. You didn't trust me and you hesitated. I don't want you to fulfill my request half-heartedly. Do it or don't do it but I don't want to twist your arm to make you do what I ask. Submissiveness is a gift that you give. It should not be forced. Forced submission is slavery and I am not trying to enslave you; I am trying to liberate you."

I don't know what to say. I don't know how to respond. I sit there like a child being scolded by her teacher.

"I'm sorry. It will not happen again," I humbly apologize. Lee was pleased.

When the band ended the song, the sax player got the microphone.

"We have a special treat for ya'll tonight. My dear friend is back in the house and she has agreed to do a spoken word piece for ya'll."

The audience clapped and cheered.

"Coming to the stage is my friend, Lee. Start clapping now as we welcome her to the stage."

My head shoots around to Lee who was looking at me like the cat that had swallowed the canary. She stood up and straightened her clothes before heading onto the stage. Picking up the mic she looks directly at me.

"The name of this piece is called, My Rayne." She announces before looking over at me and giving me a sly wink.
The crowd erupted in applause. I feel the heat rising from my neck to my face, I'm flushed. The band begins to play a sensual slow song and Lee begins to speak…

"When I met you I could see the agony in your eyes
I could feel the loneliness you felt inside
All I could think is I want to get to know her
And make it my mission to heal her hurt
Because to see your pain caused me pain
So, all I wanted to do is protect my Rayne
The first time my lips touched yours I was gone
I loved the sound of your moans
Now I can't shake the vision of you kissing me so softly
I barely feel your touch
But I want you so badly and
That slight kiss is not enough
My hand cups your breast
as I continue to kiss you on your neck
Our bodies are intertwined
and now it's hard for me to find
where my body stops and yours start
The music we make love to
is the sound of our breathing
and the beat of our heart in perfect time
I press your dress up raising it high
Rubbing my hands down your thigh
and even when you whisper a sigh
We keep our eyes locked as our bodies' rock
And sway to the music we create
There is no denying our chemistry
You are just so damn beautiful to me
Like silk, you are graceful and smooth

And I am completely lost in the essence of you
I love your gentleness, you style, your grace
I love the softness of your lips
the delicate curves of your face
I love the way you feel
the way you smell
the way you taste
I love the sensuality of your embrace
I never thought I could feel
this way about another woman
This feeling is surreal
Like a dream it seems our lips were perfectly match
Sometimes the feeling is so intense
I must catch myself
I'm so into you I can't think of anyone else
I want to feel your pussy against my tongue
Taste your juices when you cum
I love how you beg and plead
And cum almost instantly
As soon as my fingers slip past your lips
And dip into you
Making you climax over and over until I leave
You completely drained
And now it's hard for me to explain
This craving, this addiction I now have
for my Rayne"

The crowd stands to their feet, giving her a standing ovation. She graciously takes a bow.

"You are all too kind. I'm Lee, thank you and enjoy the rest of your night."

The sax player came back to the stage as Lee was walking back to our table.

"Give it up, one more time for my girl, Lee" he says.

Lee walks off the stage and kisses me on the lips in front of everyone. This is my first public display of affection with a woman and it doesn't feel strange. I'm not worried about what people are saying or thinking. It feels very natural.

My entire face is flushed. The temperature in the room has just rose 10 degrees from that poem and I was feeling the heat. I had a hard time containing myself because I wanted to touch her, to feel all those things she talked about in her poem. Lee had not licked my pussy yet. But I couldn't help but wonder what it would feel like every time I looked at her mouth. Shit!!! Ok, I need to focus on something else before I have an orgasm sitting right here at the table.

"Wow, I didn't know you did poetry," I said shaking my head in amazement.

"I dabble in it from time to time. It's just one of my hobbies."

"What other hobbies do you have?"

"Dancing is the one I love the most."

"Oh, you know I can't dance at all."

"Sure you can, everyone can dance."

"Well let me rephrase that, I can dance I just don't think anyone would want to see it. I have two left feet."

"Wrong again, you have a right and a left and nothing is wrong with either. Why are you worried about what other people think of your dancing abilities? Dancing is for the dancer. It makes you feel good. It is fun and if you are doing it from the heart you don't care what people think all you care about is how good it makes you feel."

"I guess," I replied wanting to end this conversation.

Lee jumped up, grabbed my hand and started pulling me towards the dance floor. I tried to protest but it is futile. Now I'm in the middle of the dance floor looking lost as Lee starts dancing around me. She moved behind me and put her hands on my hips. She leaned in and whispered in my ear, "We will take it slow so trust me."

"OK," I whispered back.

She holds my hips and as she sways her hips back and forth, she is forcing me to move in unison with her. I can't believe that I am on beat. When I get the rhythm good she spins me around. I continue to rock and sway my hips.

"Now when you sway to the right accent your hip movement by taking a step to the right; do the same step out when you sway to the left. Every time you come back to the middle I want you to step also"

I follow Lee's instruction and it looks like I'm dancing. It feels like I'm dancing. I'm mimicking her steps and I'm keeping up with her.

"You are doing a good job. Now, you must learn to follow my lead. If you feel my hands pushing you back, then you will step backwards. If you feel me pulling you toward me then you take a step forward. It will be the same for a spin, a dip, or a slide. You just must be in sync with your partner. Be able to read them and most of all trust your partner."

I did as Lee instructed and it didn't take long for me to get the hang of it. She was right, once I stopped caring about what others thought, dancing became fun. We stayed on the floor all night. I felt uninhibited. I felt alive, happy, and totally free for the first time in my life. As "Step in the name of love" by R. Kelly played, I morphed into a new creature.

When we left the club, I was giddy and lightheaded either from the dancing or from all the Mojitos I had downed. Either way I was feeling good. There was a difference in my stride, a noticeable sway in my hips that had never been there before. Lee took me to a hotel and then informed me that we were going to spend the night. How am I going to explain to my husband where I have been and what I've been doing all this time? I was never a cheater so coming up with lies was not my strong point. I thought for a minute then called my friend, Zola.

"Tonight, you and I went to a jazz club in Columbus. I didn't realize there was so much alcohol in the drinks and you didn't think it was safe for me to drive home so we are going to stay in Columbus," I stated matter-of-factly.

"Oh, so now we creating cover stories, are we?" Zola said sounding very amused. "You got a fine ass man at home that most women would kill for, chic. I hope he is worth it."

"Beyond worth it, trust," I couldn't keep the smile off my face.

"Well, in that case enjoy yourself and be careful. Love you, girl."

"Thanks, Love you, too."

I hung up and called Quest. He didn't answer his phone. He was probably fucking another woman anyway. I left him a short message without details and hung up. If he should call back, I didn't plan to answer the phone either. Hell, if he could do it so could I.

Quest

Since the last time Rayne caught me cheating, I had been on my very best behavior. I was keeping my promises and doing things to show her how much I loved her. She was the most important person in my life and I was so grateful that she was giving me a second chance. I wasn't going to mess this up.

I would be lying if I said it was easy. I was surrounded by beautiful women all day. The look-but-don't-touch principle just doesn't feel right. I just don't think monogamy is realistic or natural. Rayne doesn't understand that I love her and the other women are just sex. There is a difference between the two.

One of my best friend's favorite quote is, "sharing is caring." He tells me that every time I am with a woman that he would like to fuck. Open relationships don't work for some because they are still trying to live up to what society deems as appropriate.

I had a conversation recently with an ex about the three-way relationship that she was in. I asked her if it embarrassed her when she would go out with her boyfriend and girlfriend and people knew what was going on. Her response was no, what is embarrassing is to assume that your partner is faithful only to find out that he is cheating and even more embarrassing is that the people in your life knew about his cheating. The bigger betrayal to her is letting everyone in on the affair except the person you are in the relationship with. After hearing her explain her relationship, I understood more about why Rayne was so hurt when she found out other people knew I was cheating and no one ever told her.

I have talked to many women about their past relationships. Every single one of them said a man in their past (sometimes every man) had cheated on them. I asked these women what they did to make all these men cheat on them. I find it interesting that most of these women don't think they have done anything and that the men cheated because they were just greedy dogs. Well, if every man in your past has cheated on you, why would you think your current man or your future man is going to be any different? If you think all men are dogs and cheaters, then why are you hurt when it happens? You should have seen it coming, right? What is even more baffling to me is these women will find out that their man is cheating, leave him, but then keep going back for sex even after he finds another woman. I never understood why Rayne put up with me treating her like that because it wasn't like she was ugly or desperate. But if she was letting me do it then I kept doing it.

I just don't understand women. Picture this…A woman walks into a restaurant to have dinner with her group of female friends. She admits to them that her husband has cheated on her. All her girlfriends are sympathetic because they have all been in that same boat at some point in their life. They would all rally around her. Every one of them would have an opinion about what she should do. They would add her to their sisterhood of women that have been wronged by a man. There is no shock because cheating is the new normal.

Same woman walks into a restaurant to have dinner with her group of female friends. She admits that her husband brought another female home last night and she left so that they could have sex. It's not cheating because she knew all about the other woman. Her friends' reactions would be very different. She would get called stupid and asked, how could she? She would get warned about how she is inviting trouble into her home by giving a woman a chance to take her man. No sisterhood of shared stories of no good men. She would be an outcast.

I know there is no way I could get Rayne to think like this. She believed in till death do you part and that didn't involve other people. But it would be so much easier if she would realize that she is the one I love. She is the one I want and the other women are just for recreational purposes. There would be less divorces if people stopped trying to live up to the unrealistic expectations of monogamy.

I promised Rayne that she would see a changed man. I was not going to cheat anymore and so far; I had been true to my word, but it was getting harder. I told her that I would go to marriage counseling. Hell, it might even help me with my addiction to women.

I asked Siri to find a marriage counselor. The first therapist that came up was Alicia Tate. I knew her and had forgot that she did couples counseling. I viewed her webpage. I always thought she was attractive. If I am going to have to spend time looking and talking to a therapist at least she can be some eye candy. Plus, I didn't have to worry about being tempted to fuck her because she was married to my old college friend. I called her office and made an appointment to see her on Friday. I texted Rayne to let her know that I had made an appointment for us to go to counseling. I hope she can see that I am putting forth an effort to make our marriage worked.

Rayne

Lee and I are headed up to our room and the entire time we are on the elevator we are going at it like hormonal teenagers. I can't stop kissing her. Our hands are all over each other and we are both in various stages of undress by the time we reach the room.

Lee inserts the key in the card slot and opens the door. I enter first to find Simone naked and lying on our bed. I turn to look at Lee and she has a serious expression on her face so now I'm confused. Was earlier a test to see if I was open to a threesome with another woman? I'm still trying to get the hang of sex with one woman so how does she expect me to be ready to jump in bed with two women? Lee must have read my mind and knew I had so many questions.

"Go take a shower. Everything you will need is in the bathroom," Lee tells me.

I don't respond. I don't look at Simone. I just walk to the bathroom. There I find lingerie and all my personal necessities. I get in the shower and my mind is swirling. Maybe if I talk to Lee and explain that I'm just not ready for all this, she will understand. I know she wants me to submit to her but this is asking too much. I made up my mind to just tell her that I will not have a threesome with her and another woman. I finished up my shower and put on the lingerie that Lee had provided. It was a satin chemise with an empire waist. The seams accentuated my breast. The gown felt smooth like butter against my skin and I looked beautiful.

When I walked into the room I am surprised to see that in my absence, Lee had managed to get undressed and is in bed kissing on Simone. They don't even notice that I have walked back into the room. I walked up to the bed and touch Lee on the back. She stops kissing Simone and sits up on the edge of the bed. Simone is lying beside her completely naked.

"You look amazing," Lee says.

"Thank you," I reply before going off on a tangent about how I couldn't possibly do a threesome with her and Simone.

"Good," Lee replies. "I am glad you didn't want to do a threesome because that was not what I had in mind. I told you submission is a gift. I don't want you to have regrets when you give me a gift. No buyer's remorse. I don't want to demand obedience I want you to follow willingly. You can't do that and so my plan was

not to reward you for your lack of trust and obedience. Simone was obedient. I appreciate her for that and I wanted to show her how much I appreciated her. All I want from you is for you to watch."
I couldn't even speak.

"Now, go sit in that chair over there in the corner," Lee instructed.

Was I being banished to sit in a corner like the class dunce? Who does Lee think she is? I had a mind to just get my stuff and go. She was taking this submissive shit too far. Who the hell in their right mind follows another person blindly? I mean, really? I'm just supposed to do whatever she says without question, without hesitation? Who does that? I was questioning everything that happened and while doing so I walked to my chair in the corner and sat down. I didn't want to leave. As much as it bothered me for Lee to treat me this way, I couldn't walk out of that room. I had to see what happened next. I couldn't leave, so I sat in the corner and jealously watched Lee with a woman that wasn't me.

Lee got up and turned on all the lights to make sure I wouldn't miss any parts of her fucking Simone. She got back in bed and wrapped her arms around Simone and began to kiss her. I felt a sick feeling of jealousy in my belly. I didn't want to see this but I couldn't turn away. I watched Lee sucking on Simone's bottom lip. I watched their tongues intertwine. I heard Simone and Lee moaning in unison and I am going crazy.

Lee is on top of Simone. She kisses her ears and Simone's back arches. She kisses down her neck and Simone's arms and legs wrap around Lee. Lee licks and sucks on Simone's nipples and she grabs Lee's hair and moans. Every one of Lee's actions causes a reaction in Simone. By the time Lee reaches Simone's pussy her legs are already spread eagle in anticipation. Lee inserts one finger into Simone's pussy then two. Simone is grinding on Lee's fingers like they were a dick. Lee uses her free hand to pull back the hood of Simone's pussy and expose her clit. The first lick of Lee's tongue to Simone's pussy must have been a shock because she stopped moving and said, "Oh, shit."

She was still other than the twitching of her legs and the tapping of her foot in unison with each lick. I guess it took her a minute to recover because she stopped being still and started back grinding, hard! She was thrusting her pussy up toward Lee's face and holding the back of her head. I don't know how Lee didn't suffocate. I was amazed by the aggressiveness of the oral sex between the two. With Quest, everything had always been slow and sweet. Even when he ate my pussy it was always slow, gentle licks and I would stroke his bald head lovingly while he pleasured me. Watching the two of them go at it like this was confusing to me.

Simone obviously was loving what Lee was doing to her pussy. Lee was working her tongue and fingers simultaneously and Simone was screamed so loudly I was afraid that we would get reported and asked to leave the hotel. Simone let out the loudest yell and then she went from pushing Lee's head into her pussy to trying to push her head away; but Lee held onto her thighs. The more that Simone tried to get away the tighter Lee held on. Her feet were sliding up and down the bed moving her head closer to the headboard but Lee stayed with her. Finally, she could speak and begged Lee to stop for just a minute and Lee did, leaving Simone gasping for air and shaking.

Lee sat on the edge of the bed and looked at me.

"I want you to be honest with me. How did that make you feel watching us?" Lee asked.

"Jealous," I admitted.

"Why?

"Because those are the things I wanted you to do to me."

"What I do to women is a gift but I am selfish. I only give to those that give to me. Your gift to me is total submission and my gift to you is pleasure. Do you understand?"

"Yes."

"Good."

"Now Simone come around here and taste my pussy."

Simone gets up walks around the bed to where Lee is sitting. She gets down on her knees. Lee slides down to the edge of the bed and leans back propping herself up on her elbows. Simone starts eating her pussy while Lee and I maintain eye contact. After a few minutes, Lee stops her.

"Kiss Rayne," She instructs Simone.

Now, I have tasted my own pussy on my husband's lips before but never have I tasted a woman's pussy on the lips of another woman. Simone turns to me and still on her knees she lifts her wet lips up to my face. I kiss her with closed lips but she forces

84

my mouth apart with her kiss and sticks her tongue deep in my mouth. I love the sensation, the feel, the thought that we were exchanging Lee's juices.

"Eat her pussy, Simone."

Simone grabbed me and pulled my hips so that most of my ass was hanging off the chair. She put my legs on her shoulder and went to work like my pussy was her last meal. It only took two minutes for me to cum.

"Good girl, Simone. Now give me a kiss and you can head out." Simone kissed Lee and got her clothes and left.

"Come and get in the bed with me."

I got up and walked over to the bed and Lee and I spooned. No sex. She held me with her mouth nuzzled against the back of my neck until we fell asleep.

I dreamed of Lee between my legs licking my pussy. I hated her for making me watch her and Simone so in my dreams, I was the one in control. I was making Lee eat my pussy the same way that she was doing Simone. I climaxed so hard that it shook me awake. I looked down to see the top of Lee's head between my legs. I wasn't just dreaming.

"Good morning, baby." Lee says with the smile of a Cheshire cat on her face.

"It's a great morning." I purr. I am blissfully happy.

Lee takes a dildo and slides it inside my pussy before going back to work on my clit with her tongue. This is a first for me as well. I am getting fucked by a dick and getting my pussy ate at the same time. I hear angels singing so I'm sure this is heaven.

Zola

I was always of the opinion that anybody that was looking for love online was both lonely and desperate. But I had hit a dry spell. The struggle is real if you are a Black woman who wants to love a Black man. Online love was the last thing I was looking for or expected to find but here I was searching through profiles of eligible bachelors.

It's funny when you read an online profile everyone is financially secure, drama-free, well-endowed, exciting and has a great sense of humor. Bullshit! I have met a few people in person and the way they view themselves is never who they are in person. I met a 39-year-old that still had hopes of getting discovered and becoming a famous rapper. He called himself the Grave Digger because he "killed and buried sucker MC's" those are his words, not mine. Never mind the fact that this fool was still walking around with his pants sagging off his ass. In the restaurant, he takes the grill out his mouth and puts it on the table right before we get ready to eat. I excuse myself to go to the bathroom and politely walked right out the door.

Then there was the over achiever who talked about all his accomplishments. I couldn't get a word in between all his praises of himself. He was so successful, so smart, so great and wonderful but he just hadn't been able to find a woman of his caliber. He had been married 4 times but was positive that he was not the problem in his relationships. Excuse me, but I learned in math that sometimes you must locate the common denominator to solve the problem. He had 4 different wives but they all had the same husband. His theme song should be Michael Jackson's, *Man in The Mirror*.

Then there are the times when my online friend brings their representative instead of their true self. They pretend to be the person you are looking for until you get to know them and just like a chameleon they change colors and you see them in their true form. Those dates are the worse because as soon as I start feeling the great and powerful wiz of a representative, they disappear and I'm just left with the little man hiding behind the curtain.

Part of my problem is that I am only attracted to a certain type of man. I like dark skin, tall, bald head men. I joke with my brother, Tommy, about light-skin men going out of style with break dancing. I would tell him that light-skin men went out in the 80's. To which he would always reply that light-skin was making a comeback. I started thinking about how popularity is governed by the people. Eighties fashions were hideous but a lot of those same hideous fashions made a comeback by popular demand. We see it. We buy into the hype. We want it. There was a time when everyone wanted a light-skin brother with good hair. Some of those brothers took women for granted because they were a hot commodity. They could have their pick of women so they dogged out some good women. But waiting in the wings to pick up the pieces of those crumbled hearts was a dark-skin brother who not only didn't have good hair, he had NO hair. Black, bald, and beautiful and he was humble. He appreciated that woman and the balance of power started to sway and the light-skin brothers were put on the shelf like acid washed jeans and jelly shoes.

There was a shortage of good men. I read somewhere that 40% of women have never been married. That is a devastating fact to women that were brought up on the fairy tales of Prince Charming and happily ever after. The statistics increase when it comes to the number of Black women that have never married. When you look at the population of Black men and you start to take away the ones that are:

Already Married

Incarcerated

Gay/Bi/DL

Don't date Black women

That doesn't leave very many Black men to choose from. The number goes down even further if you subtract the no-good men. We are left with a minuscule amount of good Black men that are available to us. Many sisters have broadened their horizons and have started dating outside of their race. Some have opted for the if-you-can't-beat-them-join-them approach and are willingly sharing their man with another woman. Other women are taking the no-good man just so that she can have a piece of man rather than be without a man. She will swallow all his bullshit and let him tell her its steak because she is too afraid of being lonely.

No good men read the same statistics that women read. They understand that they are in high demand because there is a shortage of men. It isn't light skin vs dark skin anymore. It's the good man vs the bad man and the good men are losing out. He is on the verge of extinction. I can't tell you how many times I have heard dumb ass females (yes, I called them that) tell a man he is just too nice or he is too good for her. I just want to slap a woman when I hear that. She is telling that good man that nobody is going to want him if he is kind, sensitive, and sweet. She is running back to her old boyfriend that cheated on her and beat her. She will fight another woman for sleeping with "her" man. So, guess what the good guy does? He starts to dog women too. Because the bad dog is the one taking all the bones while the good dog is starving.

Just like the fashion world, we can control the type of men that are in style. We control it by what we are willing to accept. Just like most us refused to follow the Kris Kross fad of wearing our clothes backward; we can just say no to the no-good man. Women should get together like they did during the 70's but instead of burning their bras they should burn all their no-good man's shit.

All women are basically in competition with each other for a handful of eligible men; but we must be like a skilled fisherman, throw those little worthless fish back and wait for the prize catch. But we are so afraid that if we throw the one fish we have back in we will never catch another one. We hold on for much too long strictly out of fear.

Rayne

The minute I read the text from Quest I knew it wasn't for me.

Hey Sexy, Can I get a repeat of what you did at the club? I haven't nutted that fast since high school. You must give me a chance to redeem myself.

Sure. I text back, *what do you have in mind?*

I don't just want head, although that shit was amazing. I want to fuck, too.

Despite Quest's good husband act, I knew he hadn't changed. I knew he would never change. I'm not even mad at him anymore. I just don't give a fuck. I parked my car and I'm almost to the door when I see my neighbor, Chris outside detailing his Mercedes. He looked up at me and smiled. I had never paid him any attention before. I only had eyes for my husband so I didn't look at other men. But today, I see him. He has a beautiful dark brown complexion. He is tall with an athletic build. I knew he lived alone and there were times when I caught him watching me. I walked over to him and with no hesitation I asked him if he wanted to fuck me.
He stammered and asked me to repeat what I said.

"Do you want to fuck me?" I asked again.

"Are you trying to get me killed? What do you think your husband would do to me?"

"I'm not with him anymore. I'm single."

"When did that happen?"

"Now. Do you want to fuck me or not?"

"Yes." He finally agrees.

I grabbed him by his hand and headed towards my front door. For a brief second, I thought what would our neighbors think but that thought was soon replaced with; fuck what the neighbors think. We walked straight to the front door, I unlocked it and still holding his hand, we walk in. Initially I was going to take him to the bedroom but a part of me still respected my husband enough not to violate the sanctity of our marital bed. I lead Chris over to the sofa and pushed him down. I straddled his lap and started kissing him passionately, sucking his bottom lip between mine. He let out a moan and I become more aggressive. I grabbed his hands and put them on my ass. His dick is already swollen and pressing against the fabric of his jeans. We continued kissing while he gripped my ass forcing my pussy to grind back and forth against his erection. I climbed off him and order him to get undressed. I go into my bedroom and get some strawberry lubricant and my bullet from the drawer of my bedside table. I returned to the living room completely naked and there was Chris, sitting on the couch, his dick standing at attention.

"Do you have a condom? I asked.

He reaches into the pocket of his pants and pulled out a gold wrapped Magnum XL. I take the condom from him because I'm not ready for that yet. I get down on my knees between his legs and let the strawberry lubricant run down from the tip of his dick to his balls. Once I have enough lubricant on him, I begin to stroke his dick. The lube is to make his dick slick and help my hand glide easily up and down his shaft. I take just the head of his dick in my mouth and begin to suck while my hand continues to stroke him. His eyes are closed his head has fallen back against the sofa. His moans and my slurping are the only sounds in the room. I move my hand and slide my mouth all the way down until my lips touch the base of his dick.

"Shit!" He is sitting up now, looking down at me, his eye wide open. He is watching me take his entire dick deep in my throat. I grab the back of my hair up into a ponytail and then replace my hand with his. I show him how I want him to use my hair and his hand as a guide for my mouth. If he wanted me to suck faster all he had to do was move my head up and down faster, or he could slow it down. He was in control of the pleasure I was giving him with my mouth. He moved my head up and down in a slow pace. I had a rhythm going. My mouth would come up and my hand would come up and make a quick circle around the head of his dick before my mouth was on its way back down to the base. I continued this cycle of suck, circle, stroke, swallow until I knew he was about to cum. I stopped. Damn, sucking his dick had my pussy soaking wet.

I took the condom and ripped the package open with my teeth. Placing the condom over my tongue I put his dick back in my mouth and as my mouth went down on his dick, I rolled the condom down with my lips. I get off my knees and straddle him again. His dick was twice as thick as my hole. He pushed hard but the head still wouldn't enter. I reached down and spread pussy lips with my finger to help him. I eased myself down on his massive dick and even though my pussy is soaking wet there is still resistance. He wraps his hands around me and holding onto my ass, he lowers me down slowly; he only allowed the tip of his dick to penetrate me before he raised me back up. Each time he lowered me back down, he put a little more of his huge dick into my pussy. I feel her opening to him and the feeling is unbelievable. It was still painful but even the pain felt incredible. Chris was younger than I was but he was experienced in pleasing a woman. By the time he got his entire dick in my pussy, I was at the brink of orgasm. I planted my feet on each side of his hips, holding on to his shoulders I started bouncing up and down on his dick. Each time I would go all the way down I felt pain and pleasure simultaneously and I wanted more. I was fucking him feverously like I was on the last leg of a sprint and the finish line was just in site.

"Yes baby, right there baby, damn you hitting that spot." I screamed.
My orgasm came in such powerful waves that I lost my balance as my legs weakened and I fell forward against his chest. He stopped moving and just held onto me while my pussy continued to spasm with pleasure.

"Fuck, fuck, fuck!" I screamed unable to form any words more complicated as orgasm after orgasm shot through me.
I looked down and his entire stomach is wet with my juices.
In one movement, he pushed me to the side and stood up. Now he has me bent over the couch and is fucking me doggy style. He reached up and grabbed a handful of my hair and pulled me to him with each thrust.

"Get my phone and record this. I want to see you fucking me."

Chris picked up my phone from the end table. I never bothered to put a password on it because I never had anything to hide. I can see the glow of the light as my phone comes on.

"Baby, you are going to enjoy this view. Damn, your ass looks so good"

I am moaning with ecstasy and he is grunting, cursing and smacking my ass.

"I'm cumming, don't stop," I screamed before biting down on my lower lips.

As the peak of my orgasm subsided, I felt his dick swelling inside me. He pulled his dick out, snatched the condom off and shot hot, creamy cum all over my ass. He walked into the kitchen and returned with some paper towel to wipe off the evidence of our play time. We both sit on the couch and try to catch our breath.

"What was that about?" He questioned me.

"I just wanted to fuck but if I had known you were going to be this good, I would have fucked you a long time ago." I said with a sly smile.

"I'm just next door so you can get a repeat whenever you are ready." He winked.

"Oh don't worry, I'm going to be calling on you quite often to be my maintenance man."

"So what about Quest?"

"You don't have to worry about him." I answered sharper than I meant to. I just don't want to get into a discussion about my husband and that whole mess.

"Excuse me. Miss Lady"

"I'm sorry. It's nothing. I just don't want to talk about it. I am feeling so good now and I don't want anything to ruin this feeling."

"Ok, we won't talk about him."

"Thank you." My tone is softer now.

I stood up, got dressed and started walking to the door and Chris followed my lead.

"I'll see you again soon." I promised.

"I can't wait." He smiled before walking out the door.

As soon as he leaves out the door, I go pick up my phone and search for the video. I hit play and watch this man fuck me like porn star. I attached it to a text message and send it to Quest. The text message after the video read:

I could have cheated on you but I chose to be faithful. Now I'm telling you in my Beyoncé voice: You must not know 'bout me, you must not know 'bout me. I will have another you in a minute, matter fact he'll be back in a minute. So don't you ever get to thinking.... your irreplaceable.

By the time I sent the second text message Quest was calling my phone. I turned my phone off and went into the bathroom to take me a nice, hot bubble bath.

Quest

My cell phone went off and it was a text from Rayne. I picked up my cell phone to read her message but she had sent me a video. I clicked play and my phone played a video of Rayne getting fucked from behind by some dude. She was throwing that ass back like a pro. All I heard was the slapping of this dude slamming into my wife's ass and her moaning and screaming.

I scrolled up her messages and realized the message I meant to send to Rachel I had sent to Rayne. I knew I had fucked up but she would never fuck another man; at least that is what I thought. I don't know who this dude is but when I find him, I am going to kill him. I can't get dressed fast enough. I'm mad and hurt and confused. Fuck! I must have messed up this time. The sick feeling was creeping back into my gut. What if I had lost her forever?

I got in my car and was speeding the entire ride home. I don't know what I'm going to do when I get there. I righteously can't get mad at her as many times as I've cheated on her but still... I know women don't just fuck with their pussy, they fuck with their minds and hearts. I know part of the reason she always stayed with me no matter what was because she loved me and I had been her first lover.

When I get to the house, I see her car is gone. Fuck I don't have a key. Rayne had taken the spare key off my keychain. I had been blowing Rayne's phone up and she wasn't answering my calls or text messages. I walked around the house checking all the windows, hoping to find one that was unlocked. They were all secured and all the doors were locked. I kept trying to call her phone and she wouldn't answer. I called everyone she knew and nobody had seen her. I started wondering if she had taken her stuff. If she had packed up and left. Was she ever coming home? I was sick.

I remembered, we gave her mom a key when we went on vacation so she could check on the house for us. I got in my car and headed over there to get the key, hoping that Rayne would be there so that I could try to fix things with her. I fucked up this time, but I promise if she gives me one more chance, I'm going to do right by her.

Rayne

When I got out of the tub, I logged onto my Ashley Madison account and began to update my profile with my correct information. If Quest was going to look for hookups online then I was, too. Hell, I might even find his replacement on here. I uploaded a current picture then I waited. The first man that sent me a message was a caramel colored brother that was Fine with a capital F. His profile said that he was tall, 6'2 to be exact, truck driver, athletic and toned and that he was a Libra. The best part was that he was currently online. I sent him a message introducing myself and he answered back immediately.

Still angry and hurt from catching my husband cheating, I was bold in my flirtation. My first message was, "I know you don't know me but can you fuck me and make me forget about my husband for a minute."

His response was, "Wow."

Now I am feeling embarrassed and ashamed. He must think I am some sort of thot that picks men up on the internet all the time. I regretted sending that message and wished I could take it back.

He replied again, "It sounds more like you need a good ear instead of a good dick."

I didn't know what to say to that so I just sat there, staring at the screen.

"Your husband must have done something really horrible if you want a stranger to fuck you into amnesia."

I don't know why I found his statement amusing but I found myself staring at the words on the screen with a smile on my face.

"Are willing to give me an ear and not a dick?" I questioned.

"If that is what you need then that is what I will give you."

I thought for a minute and then asked him if he could meet me at a Starbucks that was at the halfway mark between where we lived. He agreed and we both logged off.

I went to the bathroom to freshen up my make-up before heading out to the coffee shop. This should be interesting since I've never met a person that I've talked with online. I was nervous but at the same time excited.

The coffee shop was filled with the usual patrons of college student using the free Wi-Fi, men dressed in business suits reading newspapers and soccer moms. Spotting my online friend was easy. I walked toward his table and he stood to greet me.

"Wow, you are even more beautiful in person."

Blushing, I thanked him.

"Would you like something to eat or drink?" he asked.

"I would love an espresso and cream cheese Danish." I replied.

He walks to the counter to order and I remember that I haven't eaten today. Now I'm starving so when my internet friend returns with my Danish it only takes a minute for me to devour the entire thing. My internet friend watched me eat with a slight grin on his face.

"Hungry?" he jokes.

"I'm sorry. I didn't realize I hadn't eaten all day. Today has been so stressful."

"I understand and that is why I am here. To lend you, my fair lady, a listening ear. My name is Mike by the way. The women in my life call me Big Mike." He says with a wink.

"Nice to meet you, Mike, I'm Rayne."

"A beautiful name for a beautiful woman."

I proceed to tell him about catching my husband in the act of being unfaithful. I gave him all the details up to the point of me showing up at the hotel.

Mike listened intently and when I grew silent, he started laughing. I'm pissed. Here I am pouring my heart out to him and he is acting like I just performed a comedy show. I'm ready to get up and walk out.

"I would have given anything to see the expression on your husband's face when he opened the door and saw you there. I bet that was priceless." He laughed this infectious laugh and before long I find myself laughing too. We started talking and getting to know each other and he seems like a genuine, nice guy except for the fact that he was on a site to help people cheat.

"So what's your story? Why are you looking for someone to cheat with?"

He paused for a minute and then replied, "I wasn't looking to cheat, and I was looking for companionship, a friend. If that friendship evolved into a sexual relationship, then great. But that wasn't my purpose for being on there."

"Well, I assume you are married and to me cheating starts way before penetration. People start cheating in their hearts and minds well before they cheat with their body and to me that is the worse." I replied, looking down at my coffee and feeling the tears start to sting my eyes.

"You know what is worse than cheating for me?" he asked.

"What could be worse than cheating?"

"Not feeling loved or appreciated; being taken for granted. There is nothing that I wouldn't do for my wife and in the beginning, we were each other's priority. Over time, it seemed like I mattered less and less to her. I was always the one being put on the back burner while she attended to everything and everyone else. I felt like we were roommates. We were going through the motions of being married but I might as well have been in that house alone."

There was a pain in his face that I recognized because I had felt it too. I felt neglected and I didn't feel appreciated either so I understood exactly where he was coming from. I know people get busy with their day-to-day life and you just get used to people being there so it doesn't seem special anymore. But what you did to get that person. You also must do to keep that person. You must make time to make that person feel special and that requires more than a date night once a week. Often we stop saying thank you, we stop complementing our mate and too often marriage becomes just like a job; something you do because it is expected and required. It's no longer fun and sexy, it's work.

I guess I was so deep in my own thoughts that I tuned Mike out. I didn't even notice he had stopped talking and was now staring at me.

"Earth to Rayne, come in Rayne." He jokes.

"I'm sorry. Blame my ADHD. I get distracted so easily."

"I'm hurt because I assumed that I was so suave and debonair that I had your complete attention. I guess it's true what they say about assumptions."

I apologized again. He said that he was only joking. He understood why I wasn't present with him.

"Are you ready to leave?"

I don't respond immediately. I am still thinking. I am thinking about Quest and those damn condoms on the night stand. I am thinking about that stupid fucking smile that he had on his face

97

when he opened the door to go get the fake me. I am thinking about all the times he has apologized for cheating but never stopped doing it. I am thinking about that damn text message and my mother's comforter that he fucked that bitch on. My mind goes back to the beginning when we were young and in love and I thought giving Quest my virginity was something special. He had been my first and only lover. Fuck Quest!

"I'm ready to leave but I want to go to a place where we can be more intimate."

I don't know how to say, I just want to fuck, I want you right here and now. I'm not that damn bold.

"Are you sure? I don't want you to do something you will regret later."

"We are both adults. You didn't pick me up in a bar and I'm not drunk off this espresso. I'm in my right mind and I've made a choice. I want to have sex with you."

Again, with the lady like ways. I wanted to say look, I want you to take me to a hotel, tear my clothes off and fuck me until I pass out.

"Let's go." He said and I followed him out the door and get in my car. He got into his car and I followed him. I'm not sure of our destination and for a minute I think about the horror stories of women who have met men online and then came up missing. For a second I think about turning the opposite direction but I continued following him. He didn't seem like a crazy-stalker-rapist-serial killer kind of guy. Hopefully, my intuition about him is right and I don't end up folded up in a suitcase in his trunk. He pulls into the parking lot of a Hampton Inn. I pulled in a parking space close to the door and wait for him to come back out. After getting the room keys he parked his car in a space next to mine and opened my car door.

"Are you sure about this?" he asked again.

"Yes, I told you what I wanted" I am short with him.

"Ok, I won't ask again." He throws up his hands in mock surrender."

He grabbed my hand and we head to the hotel elevator. When we got into the elevator he pressed me against the back wall and kissed me. My pussy throbbed immediately. It still felt weird that other men could make me feel the way Quest made me feel. My knees are weak and I hold on to his shoulders for support. The bell chimes when we reach our floor and the doors open. I'm still so shaken from our kiss that I continue to hold on to him. Mike takes the key card out of the envelope, slides it in the slot and opens the door.

"After you my lady."

"Well thank you kindly, young gentleman." I say in an over exaggerated southern accent.

The room is a beautiful mixture of creams, browns and green. We walk into a small living area with a sofa, tables and TV. There is one bed, a king-sized bed in the middle of the room and a desk with a mirror in the corner. Mike begins to kiss me again and I started to get undressed but he grabbed my hands.

"Leave your clothes on for now," he said in this honeyed touched baritone voice.

He raised my skirt and began to pull my panties down. I'm embarrassed because I knew they are already soaking wet. I started to protest but he quieted me with a kiss.

He led me to the bed and instructed me to sit. I followed each command like a child playing Simon says.

"Lie back." He instructed and I obeyed.

"Open your legs." I again follow his instructions

He gets down on his knees and sticks his hands under my ass and in one swoop he has pulled me to the very edge of the bed.

His face is eye level to my pussy. He kissed my clit softly. Just a sweet kiss like a boyfriend's kiss to the forehead and my eyes closed.

The next kiss was a passionate lover's French kiss. I was having an out of body experience, floating above and watching myself be devoured by this man that was eating my pussy like a plate of barbeque ribs on the 4th of July; his face slathered in my juices.

He held my pussy lips apart with one hand while the fingers of his other hand penetrated me. First one, then two, moving in and out at a slow and steady pace. My clit exposed, his tongue flickered up and down quickly then he would take these long, slow licks up and down the length of my pussy before ending with his lips softly sucking my clit into my mouth. Every time he switched his stroke, I was taken to another level of pleasure. I've never been aggressive when it came to sex but this man was bringing out this beast in me. I grabbed him by his bald head and began to grind my pussy against his tongue and lips like I saw Simone do Lee. He replaced his fingers with his tongue and the feel of his tongue inside my pussy made me cum. My movement became erratic and now that tongue on my clit was more than I could take. I tried pushing his head away but he wouldn't move. I tried to climb away from him but he wrapped his hands around my thighs and held me in place. I am shaking and can barely catch my breath. It feels so good that I'm on the verge of tears when he finally releases me. I can't move. I'm still on the edge of the bed, still trembling when he gets undressed.

"Sit up." He ordered and again, I obeyed.

He is standing in front of me. His erect dick pointing towards my mouth. I leaned forward and it brushed my lips. I am ready to take him in my mouth but he will not let me.

"You have to tell me what you want." He says with authority.

"I want you in my mouth." I replied.

"That's not good enough. I need you to tell me exactly what you want to do and you need to ask nicely."

"I want to suck your dick, please." I said getting turned on by the boldness of my statement.

"That's a good girl. Now you can put my dick in your mouth."

I opened my mouth and twirled my tongue around just the head of his dick. I feel it swell.

I rubbed my tongue down the entire length of his dick. I hear him moan. Now it's my turn to do him like he did me. I started with the head and inched my way down the entire shaft of his dick until it disappears into my throat. I hear his moan again followed by a barrage of fucks and damns. I got him now. He is deep in my throat and I can hear the slight gag that I know produces the thick spit that I'm going to need to give him a proper blow job. I pulled him out of my mouth and allowed cum-like spit from deep in my throat to coat his dick. It's sloppy and wet and now it glides in and out of my mouth with ease. I used the spit as lubricant for my hand. As my mouth comes up to the head, my hand also moves up making a small circle around the head of his dick before both mouth and hand go back down to his balls. My other hand is wrapped around him touching his ass. With each stroke of my hand the other hand pushes his ass so that his hips move forward to meet my mouth. I had never enjoyed sucking a dick this much.

His dick was in my throat, going down further than I thought possible. My eyes watered and my mascara ran streaming black tears. After a few minutes, he snatched his dick away and pushed my head a way.

"Shit, are you trying to make me cum?" He tried to fight me but I was not giving up. He is going to give me what I'm craving. He cups the back of my head and his muscular thighs shuddered with excitement before he unloaded into my mouth. I give him a minute to recover before I put a condom on him and walk over to the desk. I want to watch him fuck me. I want to be able to look into his eyes while he is deep inside my pussy. His dick fit perfectly in my pussy and watching him intensified the sensation. I am so lost in the moment that I close my eyes and lie my head down on the desk only to have him grab my hair in the front and pulled me back up; forcing me to look at him the entire time. He is sexy as fuck. I am biting my lip between my teeth while he is looking at me in the mirror, I was trying to hang on to some composure but the feeling was overwhelming.

"Oh God, Oh God, yessss!" I screamed in orgasmic bliss.

"That's right baby, that's who you are fucking right now. Call me by my name" He is arrogantly cocky and I love it.

"I am your God and you are my beautiful Goddess."

I continued to have orgasm after orgasm until my legs felt like Jell-O and I could no longer stand. This man was amazing and I was going to put him on my roster. He could get it whenever he wanted it. Revenge fucks were fun and I planned on having a lot more fun.

Chris

Having a threesome with a woman and another dude never appealed to me but I would do anything for Rayne. She was so sexy and beautiful. I knew I had to keep my feelings in check when dealing with her, after all, she was married. But that dog didn't deserve her. He didn't treat her right. He had a good woman at home but was always out fucking around. Honestly, I was just waiting around, hoping that eventually she would get tired of his shit and give me a real chance. But until then, I was just enjoying my time with her.

We were lying in bed one night after an exhausting sex session when we started talking about fantasies. Even though Rayne is older, she hadn't experimented much. She married Quest when she was young and up until recently, he had been her only lover. I understood why she wanted to try new things and spread her proverbial sexual wings. Although, I didn't want to even think about another man touching her, let alone seeing that shit in person; I wanted to make her happy. I wanted to make her fantasies come true.

Tonight, I planned to make at least one of my beautiful neighbor's fantasies come true. My friend, Seven, had agreed to take part in a threesome for Rayne. It wasn't the first time that Seven and I had shared a woman. We used to do it in college back when the running theme was, "it ain't fun if the homies can't have none." Back then it was just random ass girls, most of which we either didn't bother to learn their names or soon forgot them. But I had real feelings for Rayne.

Seven and I had smoked a blunt and had a few drinks. The plan was that he was going to hide in my closet. I kept the door cracked. I would leave enough light on in the room so that he could watch. Once, Rayne and I got going then he would come out the closet and join me in pleasuring Rayne. I kept telling myself that no matter what, I had to keep my feelings in check.

The doorbell rang and I went downstairs to let her in. It was raining outside and even though Rayne was drenched, she was still sexy as hell. I let her in and took her to the bathroom first. I undressed her, stripped off her wet clothes and towel dried her gorgeous body. I held her hand and led her to the bed. She was lying on her back and I kneeled beside her head so she could suck my dick while I finger-fucked her pussy. I was afraid that if Seven walked out of the closet, Rayne might get startled and bite my dick off. I pulled out of her mouth.

"I have a surprise for you." I said and motioned for Seven to come out of the closet.

"What is this?" Rayne questioned.

"Your fantasy," I responded back. "Trust me."

Seven went to the foot of the bed and came up between Rayne's thighs, burying his face in her pussy. She reacted immediately with an arch of her back, her mouth fell open in a silent gasp. Jealousy shot through me. Rayne put my dick back in her mouth and with every moan of pleasure she pulled me deeper into her mouth. Jealousy disappeared.

I replaced my dick with a finger in her mouth so that I could suck on her nipple while Seven continued licking her pussy. Seven came up and took her other nipple in his mouth. We both sucked her nipples at the same time while Seven fingered her to orgasm.

"Get on your knees." I instructed her.

She obliged.

I fucked her from behind while she is giving Seven head. I am trying to focus on how good her pussy feels instead of this nigga fucking Rayne's mouth. I could tell Rayne was enjoying everything that we were doing so that made me feel better. But shit, I needed to get out of my head. I was doing this for her and I needed to make sure that her fantasy lived up to the hype.

"I want you to ride Seven." I told Rayne.

She quickly mounted Seven and began to slow wind on top of him. I got the lubricant from the nightstand and put some on my dick. I rubbed lubricant on her ass and slid my finger in and out of her ass. I felt her tense.

"I've never had anal sex before." Rayne admits.

"Trust me." I respond back.

I placed the head of my dick against her asshole and rubbed it in small circles. Rayne moaned and I felt her start to relax. I pressed against her tight opening and felt it give slightly. I moved just the head of my dick in and out of her ass very slowly. Rayne's moans grew louder. She leaned all the way forward and kissed Seven exposing her ass completely to me. This time I don't withdraw, I just continue pushing forward and I feel her ass opening to accommodate me. She is cumming already. I can feel the spasms in her asshole. She released a loud scream her body quivered. She takes a few minutes to recover and starts back fucking us both until the three of us cum.

We fuck all night, Rayne and I, Rayne and Seven and the three of us together, until we are dog-tired. When Seven leaves, Rayne and I, hold each other into a blissful stupor.

"Thank you." She kisses me.

"You don't have to thank me."

"Yes, I do. That was the most unselfish thing you could have done for me. Quest is all about what feels good to Quest. He never considers my feelings and what I want. He would have never put my needs above his."

"I want to make you happy, Rayne. I want you, not just sex. I want all of you. I love you Rayne. I kept thinking this was just infatuation but infatuation is blind. Love is all-see and accepting. I can see your blemishes and I accept them. I recognize your fears and insecurities and I want to comfort them. I want to show you what it feels like to be appreciated. I would never take you for granted. Quest is with you but that doesn't mean that he wants to be there, it doesn't mean that he loves you. Sometimes people are just there because it's convenient. I will love you. I will dive headfirst into the depths of your stormy soul and drop anchors to keep you from being swept away to sea. I will love you in all the ways you deserve to be loved and then I will love you even more. I just need for you to give me a chance and let me prove it to you."

I felt the wetness on my chest. I knew that Rayne was crying. She didn't say anything. She just looked up at me and kissed me softly on the lips.

Quest

Rayne's scream startled me awake. I had fallen asleep and didn't hear her when she came home. She obviously wasn't expecting to see me in our bed when she returned from wherever the hell she had been all night. Because I was drinking, Baylor drove me home and I left my car parked at his house. I'm sure if Rayne had known I was here waiting on her she would not have come home. She had already showered and was standing in the doorway of our bed room.

"Where the hell have you been? I've been waiting on you all night. You aren't answering my phone calls or text messages. Your mom hadn't seen you. I called all your friends. I thought something had happened to you. I was worried. Rayne. You scared me." I couldn't stop my voice from trembling.

"When did you start to worry? Did you worry when you were at the hotel?" Rayne shot back.

"Baby, I know I messed up. I know I keep fucking up but this time I swear it will be different. I was mad when you sent me that video but then I thought after all I had done to you; how could I get mad when you finally say enough is enough? Trust me baby, I hear you. I am willing to do whatever it takes. We can go to couple's therapy. I will get counseling. Whatever you need me to do to fix this, I am willing to do. I just don't want to lose you, Rayne. I love you."

I had never allowed anyone to see me vulnerable. I was the one always in control but I was hurting. Rayne walked over and hugged me. I exhaled a deep sigh of relief. I was relieved that she didn't just curse my ass out and tell me to leave.

I bent down and kissed her and she responded like she had been waiting for me. We got undressed and I got in on my side of the bed. I patted the bed for her to get in beside him.

"Hell no, Quest Harrison, you are no longer in charge of what goes on in our bedroom. Those days of me being docile are over." Rayne marches to my side of the bed and tells me to sit up. I am surprised.

"Sit up, now!" She repeated with more authority in her voice.

I swing my legs over and sit up on the side of the bed. Rayne gets down on her knees between my legs and start sucking my dick. I let out a moan and close my eyes. This is NOT the suck-a-few-seconds-get-his-dick-hard-and-then-fuck-missionary routine that we had been doing for years. She grabbed my hand and put it on her head and made me force her head down. My dick is going so far in her throat that it is cutting off her air and making her eyes water. I have never seen Rayne so aggressive

"Wait baby, ohhh Wait. Shit, oooh you awwww shit you are going to, oh my god, make me cum." My voice is raspy and my speech is coming out in broken words mixed with moans and profanity. She had never allowed me to cum in her mouth but this time she was going to stop me. This was a fight for her and she wasn't stopping until she claimed her prize.

Finally, I let out a scream and held on to her head. Hot cum shot into her throat and she swallowed it in one gulp. She kept me in her mouth until I start to swell all over again. When I am good and hard, she tells me to lie back. I am still on the edge of the bed with my feet touching the floor. She positioned herself between my legs, facing the wall and sits down on my lap. Her pussy is already wet so I slide in easily. She started bouncing up and down on my dick using the wall to steady herself while ride a modified cowgirl. She grabbed my hands and put them on her hips so I could pull her down as I thrust upward. Damn, this feels marvelous. She is no longer the pussycat in the bedroom, she is a tigress.

"Why are you fucking me like you are scared of this pussy Quest? I bet you don't fuck those other bitches like this." Rayne says in a harsh tone that I've never heard come out of her before. She continued talking crazy to me and I'm trying not to let her get in my head.

"See that is why I had to go get some real dick. You don't know how to fuck me for real. I need a man to take charge. You saw the man in the video was fucking me right."

I stopped moving and let go of her hips before I pushed her off my dick and stood up. I grabbed her, turned her around and bent her ass over the bed. I shoved my dick roughly into her pussy.

"Owwwww" she screams.

"Don't cry now, bitch. This what you wanted ain't it? For me to fuck you like I do them random bitches?"

"Yesss!" she moaned.

"You know this is my pussy and you let that motherfucker in my pussy? Bitch, I'm going to leave you so sore you won't want another dick inside you. Hell, you won't be able to handle a finger in that pussy when I get done with you."

I grabbed her hips and yanked her to me roughly every time I thrust forward.

"Fuck! I don't know if you are hitting cervix, uterus, or stomach but you can't go any further inside me. Please, Quest. I'm sorry." She cries.

"This is my pussy, bitch. Do you hear me?"

"Yessss!" She screamed.

"Tell me. Bitch tell me this is my pussy." I demanded.

"This is your pussy Quest. It's all yours."

"Naw, talk shit like you were when you were riding me. You wanted to be aggressive then. Talking shit to me like I couldn't satisfy you. Your ass ain't fucking talkative now are you? You can't say much with all this dick up in you."

"I am cumming, black motherfucker, don't stop!" She is beyond the point of no return as spasms take control and her body shakes with pleasure.

"Bitch!!!" I scream right before I feel a load of hot cum shooting inside her.

Exhausted we lie in bed with our limbs wrapped around each other. I am blissfully happy and all is forgiven. It only took one good fuck for us to get back together.

Zola

Online dating worked great if you were looking for quantity over quality. I had gone on a lot of dates but none were what I would consider a success. I even went and bought Steve Harvey's book because I thought maybe I was doing something wrong. Steve said, sometimes as women we must lower our standards. I thought that was some bullshit. What's wrong with standards? But since I haven't had any luck, I thought what the hell. I went out on dates with guys that I would normally have laughed at if they had the nerve to ask me out. Even those had ended in disaster.

This date tonight, just feels different. The brother seemed to have his shit together. He was a gentleman. He showed up with flowers and opened my car door. He was funny, extremely intelligent and fine as hell with an Idris Elba sort of sexiness that made my juices flow.

Steve Harvey would be so disappointed in me right now. In his book, he told women to make men wait. He said to make them work for the cookies. Before we got back to my house, my plan was to keep my cookies in the jar for at least 90 days; but now, 90 minutes' feels like too long of a wait. So here I am in the bathroom trying to stop this throbbing between my legs. I figured if I could masturbate and have an orgasm then the desire to go into my living room and fuck this man I just met would wane. I'm in the bathroom with my fingers pressed deeply in my clit rubbing it harder and faster, I need to cum so bad, then my date knocked on the door.

"Are you ok?" my date asked.

"Hmmmm ohhhh yes" I replied.

"Are you feeling ok? I was getting worried about you."

Damn his talking was fucking up my flow. I guess I am not going to cum before I have to face him.

"I'm fine, I'll be out in a minute." I screamed from the other side of the bathroom door.

Now I am super horny and even more ready to fuck and this man that I've known for less than 4 hours is waiting on me to come out of the bathroom. I already know, I'm not going to be able to stop looking at the bulge in his pants that I noticed earlier. I walked into the living room and sat on the opposite end of the sofa, pussy still throbbing. I grabbed the pillow and put it on my lap.

"Are you ok?" He asked me again.

"Yes, why do you keep asking me that?"

"Because you are rocking like that."

I didn't even realize that I was rocking back and forth. No I wasn't nervous, the rocking created friction on my pussy from my panties and I was trying to get some damn relief.

I am staring at this fine ass man in front of me. Looking at his lips and wanting to bite on his bottom lip while he was fucking me. Shit! Fuck Steve Harvey! What the hell did he know anyway? The bastards been married three times and cheated on his wife. I was about to bust this jar wide open and give this motherfucker all my fucking cookies. I walked over to him, straddle his lap and took that bottom lip between my teeth. I could feel his dick swell underneath me. We may not have a second date but tonight all I was worried about was stopping the ache between my thighs.

Rayne

I didn't think Quest was serious about the whole therapy thing. It kind of surprised me when I got a text saying not only had he found a therapist he had already made us an appointment to see her this Friday. We had been getting along since we got back together. Quest was trying his best to do everything to show me how much he had changed. He was attentive and sweet. It was nothing for him to cook for me and he brought me flowers and gifts for no reason at all.

Having Lee in my life was helping my marriage. I stopped worrying about where Quest was and what he was doing. In fact, the more he stayed gone the easier it was for me to spend time with Lee. When I was at home, I was in a much better mood.

The only thing I didn't like about Lee is how she was always testing me. I didn't understand it. It didn't feel like she was doing it to hurt me but I couldn't understand why she kept doing it. Anyway, I was so intrigued by her and how she made me feel that the trials were worth it. When Friday came, Quest was too happy to go to counseling which made me suspicious.

"I know you promised to go to counseling and I see you are really trying but why are you so excited about going to see a therapist?"

"I found a therapist that I know so I think it will make things go smoother."

"Oh is this therapist a female?"

"Yes she is."

"A pretty female?"

"What does that matter, Rayne? I only have eyes for you, but yes, she is pretty. I didn't choose her because of her looks. I chose her because she really is the best."

My mind went straight to Quest cheating. I wondered if he had fucked this woman. How messed up would it be if he had me sitting there telling all the dirty, little secrets of our marriage to a woman he had fucked? I didn't want to go but Quest was doing this for me, to prove that he had changed. I put my reservations to the side and rode with him to the therapist office. We arrived a little early and check in with her receptionist who was stunningly beautiful. I wonder if Quest knew that when he made the appointment. It didn't take long before the receptionist returned and said, "Follow me, the doctor will see you now."

We get up and follow her to a room in the back of the building.

"Please, take a seat, Dr. Tate will be with you in a minute." The receptionist said before heading back to her desk. A few minutes passed before the therapist walked in and Quest was right, she was beautiful. She walked up to us and extended her hand.

"Mr. and Mrs. Harrison. I am Alicia Tate. Pleased to meet you." She says.

"I know you." Quest spoke up. "You probably don't recognize me because the times I come to visit your husband, we are usually down in his man cave." Quest explained.

"Oh, I see." Dr. Tate replies.

Ok, so Quest had not fucked her. He was friends with her husband. At least there was one woman around that I knew my husband hadn't screwed, yet. I looked up at her as she began to discuss our initial treatment plan. I realized that I knew her, too. Alicia Tate was Lee. My mouth dropped open and Lee realizing I recognized her, gave me a quick wink.

The transformation was like day and night. Gone was the bass in her voice. Gone was the sexy male swagger that I was so attracted to. The woman in front of me was Lee but at the same time she wasn't Lee. As Alicia, she was very feminine, soft spoken, conservative and professional. Her hair was flat iron straight and the fell in loose curls down her back. She had on full makeup including eyelashes. She had a dress on that accentuated her curvy body. Plus, she was wearing stilettos. I know she said she could clean up when she needed to be feminine but, damn! She was gorgeous. I had trouble focusing through our initial meeting. I could already feel my juices flowing and my panties sticking to me. Damn, why didn't I put on a panty liner? First chance I got, I planned to go to the bathroom, slip my soaked panties off and stick them in my purse.

"Tell me what brings the both of you into my office? Dr. Tate asked.

"We are trying to save our marriage." Quest spoke first.

"Is saving your marriage a desire that is mutual between you and your wife?"

"Yes, what type of question is that? Of course, she wants to save our marriage too."

Dr. Tate looked me in my eyes for the first time since she entered her office.

"Mrs. Harrison, is it your desire to save your marriage?

"Ummm," I hesitated. Shit! My husband shot me a no-this-bitch-didn't-have-to-think-about-it look.

"Yes, Dr. Tate, I want to save my marriage." I tried to sound confident in my reply.

"Great, therapy only works if both parties are mutually committed to their marriage and to seeing the therapy process completely through till the end. There will be exercises and homework that I will ask you to do. Some of the things I ask you to do may seem useless and even unorthodox but you must trust that there is a method to my madness. Can I get a commitment from both of you today?"

"Yes," We both spoke in unison

"Good, we can get started," Dr. Tate said with a smile. She handed us both pretty burgundy leather bound journals and pens.

"This is your marriage diary. You are not to sneak and read each other's diaries. If there is something in your diary that needs to be shared, we will do it during our weekly sessions.

"Weekly? I can't come here every week. My schedule just will not allow that." Quest spoke up.

"My program requires a high level of commitment. If you are not willing to give an hour a week of your time to salvage your marriage, then I question how truly valuable your marriage is to you.

"Ok, I'll do it." He finally agreed.

"Good, I will have my secretary set your next appointment. Your homework for next week is simple. I want you to write your list of the top 5 things you love about each and the top 5 things you don't like or would change. This assignment only works if you are totally honest. We don't need the politically correct answers in here. I need both of you to commit to giving and receiving the truth no matter how painful."

We both nod in agreement. I must admit that I wasn't too interested in working on my marriage but I was interested in seeing this side of Lee. I have never looked at a woman sexually. When I was with Lee it was different. Even though she was all woman, I just got used to her in that male role. Now, Alicia Tate, has me confused. There is nothing masculine about her and yet I was still turned on. I always thought I was only attracted to men and the reason I could have sex with Lee was because of how masculine she looked and acted.

Lee wrapped up our session and told us to make a follow up appointment with her secretary. We got up to leave out with Quest in the lead and I was sandwiched in between them. Before I made it out the door, Lee's hand grabbed a handful of my ass. Ms. Millie started throbbing immediately. She had me sprung. I wanted to stay behind and fuck her on that chaise lounge, she had in her office. If nothing else, going to therapy just got interesting.

Giselle

Life has become so complicated since city and states became the bathroom police. Every time I go out now, I dread going to the bathroom for fear that I might go to jail. I don't know why people thought because I was transgender, I was some sort of degenerate waiting in the dark to molest their children. I am transgender and not a pedophile. Truth be told the bigger danger to little boys were the men that looked straight, the ones that had a right to be in the men's room with little boys. Those are the ones that are looking for a child to molest. I've had this discussion so many times with people that can't seem to separate the two. Pedophiles like children. It has nothing to do with being homosexual or heterosexual.

Egypt and I were out having dinner and my bladder was so full, I thought I would just burst. There was no holding it till I got home. I had to go. Considering the last time that I ventured into the men's room, my adventure ended in a fist fight and a trip to jail, I wasn't about to make that mistake again.

There was one other person in the women's bathroom so I went into the stall to handle my business. As I'm finishing up there is a knock on the stall door and I hear a man's voice telling me to come out of the bathroom.

"Damnit man", I thought to myself. "Here we go with this bullshit again."

"I'll be right out." I say, attempting to raise my voice several octaves.

When I opened the door, I see the woman that was in the bathroom when I walked in. She found a big burly ass cop to come in the bathroom and save her from the scary transgender.

"May I help you officer?" I say in a syrupy sweet tone.

"It's against the law for a man to enter a female bathroom" He replies in a gruff voice.

"So why are you bothering me?" I was starting to get pissed.

"Do you have Identification on you?"

"No, I don't."

"If you can't show me some identification then I'm going to take you to jail."

"I don't have any"

"Turn around and put your hands behind your back. You are under arrest." He ordered.

"This is just some foolishness. Child, I am having dinner with my husband. I am not about to let you embarrass me by taking me out of the bathroom in handcuffs when I have done nothing wrong." I say before heading out of the bathroom and walking towards Egypt.

The officer grabbed me by my arm and yanked me back so hard that I fall on the ground. Egypt jumped up and ran towards me to help me up.

"What's your problem man? You didn't have to do her that way?" My mild-mannered love is beyond angry.

The policer officer pulls out his gun and points it at Egypt.

"Step back, now" He screams.

"So you going to point a gun at me? What the fuck is wrong with you man? This is police brutality. I tell you what. I am going to record this so everyone can see how you are treating us." Egypt reached into his pocket to pull his cell phone out.

The bullet struck him in the center of the chest.

Time stopped. For a minute, no one moved. I don't even remember breathing before I heard my own scream.

Egypt looked down at the hole in his chest, he looked at the officer, dazed and confused. He fell to his knees before falling forward.

I can't form words. I just scream. I grab my husband and hold his head in my lap. He is not breathing. Blood is pouring from the hole in his chest. I am trying to apply pressure. I'm trying to keep his life from seeping from the wound in his chest but blood just keeps oozing through my fingers. The ambulance arrived and the paramedics started working on resuscitating Egypt. He is loaded in the ambulance and as I was about to get in the back with him the officer grabbed my arm and tells me I'm under arrest.

"My husband is dying and you are going to be an asshole and take me to jail over using the bathroom?" I am livid. I am screaming and cursing but nothing stops this ass from handcuffing me and putting me in the back of his squad car.

We get to the jail and he books me in. Of course, I call Lee, again. I tell her that Egypt has been shot and that he is at the hospital and I was in jail. She said she was on her way and hung up. The entire time I was in jail, I thought about my husband. I wondered if he was ok. I pleaded and begged the Lord of my father, to please save my man.

When Lee came to get me, we drove straight to the hospital. I asked the nurse what room was Egypt Jones in. She looked at her computer and then at me and told me to wait for just a minute. She walked to the back and talked to another woman in a white jacket. The other woman walked towards me and asked me what relationship I was to Mr. Jones.

"I am his wife. Where is he? Is he ok?"

"If you would like to sit in the waiting room, the doctor will be out to speak to you shortly." The woman said.
I could look at her face and I already knew whatever the doctor was going to tell us was not going to be good news.

The doctor walked into the room and introduced himself. He didn't want to make eye contact but whatever he said to me he was going to have to look me in my eyes to tell me.

"Mrs. Jones, I'm so sorry. We did all we could for your husband but he lost too much blood. I'm sorry but he didn't make it." The doctor offered his condolences.

I was numb. I didn't cry. I just sat there, staring.

"You can stay in here if you like and again, I am sorry for your loss." The doctor excused himself from the room.

I hadn't felt Lee's arm around me. I hadn't heard his soft sobs. When the shock wore off, I told Lee that I wasn't ready to talk to anyone or think about arrangements. I just wanted to get away from that hospital.

"You can stay with me if you like"

"Thank you, I would like that very much."
We leave the hospital with my Egypt.

Alicia

Somehow when I walked into my office and saw Rayne, I could hold my composure. Even though Quest and Baylor had been friends for years. I didn't spend much time with him. Usually they would go to the basement and stay for hours. At first I thought they might have been lovers, so I questioned Baylor about it.

"Is Quest one of the men you slept with in college?" I asked.

"No, he is a friend."

"Are you two having sex?"

"No, he is just a friend." Baylor repeated. "Alicia, I have never been with a man or another woman since we have been together. You are my soulmate. You are everything I could hope for in a wife and I wouldn't jeopardize that for anyone." Baylor looked hurt.

"I'm sorry baby. I'm not accusing you of being a cheater. You are so accepting of my lifestyle and you allow me to do what I want to do. I just wanted you to know that if that is something you desire then we can talk about it. I wouldn't be upset and I wouldn't leave. We are soulmates and you make me happy. I want to make sure that you are happy, too." I tell him looking in his eyes and hoping he sees the sincerity in what I'm saying.

"I love you and I want you to be happy. You being with another woman doesn't bother me at all. It never has. You have never neglected your duties as a wife so your extracurricular activities don't bother me. But I have no desire to be with anyone other than you. You are the best so why would I want a Kia when I already have a Bentley?

"Did you really just compare me to a car?" I laughed.

Baylor laughed too and pulled me to him. He wrapped his arms around me and kissed my forehead.

"I love you, Alicia."

"I love you, Baylor."

We are quiet for a minute and then I started thinking about my therapy session today.

"Your friend, Quest, came to my office today for counseling and I had the opportunity to meet his wife."

"Good, I'm glad he is finally taking his vows seriously. He has a good wife but he keeps cheating. I have tried so many times to talk to him. Maybe, he gets it now. I'm proud of him for taking that first step."

"There is a slight conflict with me being their marriage counselor."

"Why? Because we are friends?"

"No, because I've been fucking his wife."

Baylor sits straight up in the bed and turns on the bedside lamp. He looks at me to see if I am joking but soon realizes that I am being serious.

"Wow! I knew you had a new female friend but I would have never guessed that it was Rayne. I didn't know Rayne was bisexual. I knew she was a virgin when she married Quest and he was the only man she had ever been with but I had no idea that she was into women"

"As far as I know I am her first and only woman. I've been with a lot of women but Rayne is special. I actually have feelings for her."

"Bae, you know this can be some dangerous waters that you are treading here. You can't carry on an affair with the wife of a couple you are providing counseling to. You are going to put your career and everything you have worked for in jeopardy."

"I know that, Baylor. I wasn't going to continue to see her. I just don't know how to break it to her. That husband of hers has taken her down through there. Now here I come bringing her even more heartache.

"I understand, but you don't have much of a choice. I know you will do the right thing."

Rayne called me the very next morning. She was not weirded out by the therapy thing. I think she was amused that she could hide a secret lesbian affair from her husband. I asked her to meet me at my house tonight and she quickly agreed.

Tonight, I wasn't going to meet her as Lee but as Alicia. I just thought it would make it easier if she didn't see me as her lover, Lee and instead saw me as Alicia her therapist.

Rayne arrived right on time. I opened the door and there she was smiling until she looked up and sees Alicia not Lee.

"Well, it's different seeing you dressed like this. You have on makeup and everything." Rayne said as she walked past me and immediately headed to my bedroom.

I grabbed her hand and stopped her.

"Rayne, please sit on the couch. I need to talk to you."

We sit on the couch and I immediately launched into my explanation of why it would not only be unethical for me to continue seeing her as a client but it could cost me my license.

"We will just find another therapist." She stated matter-of-factly.

"It's not that simple. Even if you get a new therapist, we still couldn't see each other. I know your husband. He is friends with my husband."

"You're married?"

"Yes, Rayne, I told you from the beginning that I was bisexual."

"But you didn't tell me you were married!!"

"What difference does it make that I am married, so are you." I say. I'm a little confused by her reaction.

"Because if I had known you were married then I would have known that this was just a fling for you. I have feeling for you and I thought you felt the same way."

"I do have feeling for you but even that has limitation. I may have feeling for you but I love my husband and he will always be my priority. Nobody can ever come between us." I say sternly.

"Well, thank you for being so honest." Rayne is in tears as she heads to the door.

"Rayne, I'm sorry. I didn't mean to hurt you." I apologize.

She doesn't respond. She doesn't look back. She goes to the door opens it and walks away.

Rayne

I feel like such a fool. I had fallen for Lee or Alicia, whatever the fuck her name was. I should have asked more questions instead of making assumptions. I never saw a man around. I had been to her house so many times and I didn't see any signs of a husband. But then again, I wasn't looking for a husband either. What is wrong with me? Every time I care about someone they let me down. I am so tired of getting hurt. I don't want to do this anymore. Sure, Quest has always been a cheater but he was trying and I know he loves me. He took the initiative to get us into therapy. Maybe I should stop doubting him and just focus on repairing my broken marriage.

I decided to stop by the club and tell him the truth about my relationship with Lee. If we were going to have a fair shot at salvaging our marriage, then I needed to be honest with him. I needed to come clean and confess to him that I have been having an affair and surprise it is with our new therapist. I don't know how he was going to react but we needed to tell each other the truth about everything; put it all on the table and leave it there so that we can have a fresh start.

I walked into the club and headed to the back where Quest's office was located. I opened the door and there was Quest with his pants down around his ankles and a blond haired white girl on her knees sucking his dick. He saw me and pushed her to the side. I turned around to leave and I heard him shouting my name and fumbling around to fix his clothes. I'm walking out as fast as I can. Tonight, could not get any worse. By the time I reached my car, Quest had caught up with me and stood in front of my car door.

"Rayne, I'm sorry." Quest apologizes.

"You are so right, Quest. You are the sorriest piece of man that I have ever met. Get the fuck away from my car so that I can leave."

"You know how much I have been trying. I just made a mistake, baby." Quest continues pleading his case.

"No, Quest you didn't make a mistake. A mistake is picking up cream-style corn when you meant to get whole kernel. You didn't make a mistake. You don't accidently stick your dick in another woman's mouth. You are a liar and a cheat and I was a fool to stay with you so long. You are never going to change and you know what? I don't care anymore. I realize that sometimes we just outgrow people and relationship and we must move on. I'm leaving you and I'm never coming back."

"You don't mean that Rayne. You are just upset. Baby we have always been able to work through our problems. I'll call Alicia and see if we can come in sooner than our next scheduled appointment."

"Oh yeah, about the therapist. She and I have been fucking so she can no longer be our therapist. And you know the video I sent you of me fucking another man? Well, I'm still fucking him and he is not the only man that I fucked. Baby, while you were out there doing you, I was doing me, too."

"So you are a liar and a cheat, too?"

"I learned from the best." I shoot back. "Now get the fuck away from my car and go back to that white bitch that was sucking your dick. She can have you because I don't want you anymore."

Quest stepped to the side but he doesn't say anything. He is dumbfounded. I get in the car and I think about the scene from the Five Heartbeats when Eddie King. Jr asked Flash, how does it feel to be me? It's about time Quest knew what it felt like to be deceived, lied to and cheated on. I hope he was hurting just like he had hurt me so many times in the past.

I drove straight home, parked my car and walked to my neighbor's house. Chris was always happy to see me and seeing him always made me feel better. He understood me and knew that sometimes I didn't want to talk about my problems or about life in general. I just wanted to fuck and he was happy to oblige.

He opened the door when I knocked and I walked straight past him and up the stairs to his bedroom. He followed behind me and we both removed our clothes as we climbed the stairs. By the time we make it to the bed we are naked and kissing. I drop down to my knees and take his dick into my mouth and it gives me life. He is the medicine that I needed. He is holding my head steady as he thrust back and forth fucking my mouth.

"Stand up." He ordered when he has had all he could take.

I stand up and he bends me over the bed. He grabs my ass, spreads my cheeks and buries his tongue deep inside. He sticks a couple of fingers in my pussy while he continues licking my ass and within a minute, I am screaming as wave after wave of orgasmic bliss pounded into me. He walked around to the other side of the bed and got in on his back. I straddled his face and leaned forward so that I could put his dick in my mouth while I rode his face. We continued in the 69 position until I cum again.

He rolled me over so that we are in the missionary position. He puts the head of his dick against the opening of my pussy. Even though we have had sex many times before, I still had not adjusted to his size. He gets the head in before he is met with resistance. He is gentle, giving her a chance to open to him through slow and shallow thrusts. She responded to him and I could feel her opening, relaxing as he pushes into me deeper. He is close to having his entire dick in my pussy. He kisses me passionately as he gives me the final thrust and my pussy opens completely. I am in ecstasy.

Quest

Deep down I knew that eventually Rayne would get tired of putting up with my bullshit. But there was also the arrogant part of me that thought no matter what she would never go anywhere, at least not for long. I can't even explain why I continued to fuck around even though I had a good woman at home. I was happy with Rayne, I just felt the need to conquer, to hunt. Sex with other women was a sport for me and I was the real MVP.

Rayne didn't waste any time. Within a day she had changed her phone number and the locks on the house. She emptied out our checking account and put the money in her own account. She took my clothes to my mom's house and threw them in her front yard. She blocked me on Facebook, Instagram, Snapchat, hell I couldn't even send her an email. I knew if I could just get her to talk to me that she would forgive me and everything would go back to normal.

I was lost without her. I couldn't eat. I couldn't sleep and as much as I loved women, I didn't want sex anymore. All I wanted was Rayne. I knew I didn't deserve another chance and even though I had made promises in the past and broke them, I would never mess up again. Rayne wasn't going to take my bullshit anymore. She had made that clear. I couldn't lose her. She was everything to me.

I sat outside the house waiting for her to come out. I figured she would be less likely to make a scene if I approached her at a public place. I waited on her to come out to leave and I was going to follow her and make her talk to me. When Rayne finally came outside instead of going to her car she walked down the driveway and across the sidewalk to our neighbor's house. She knocked and when Chris opened the door the two of them start kissing, right there, for everyone to see. She was fucking our neighbor. He grabbed her by the ass and pulled her into the house, shutting the door behind him.

I can't believe she would disrespect me like this. How could she fuck our neighbor? I looked at the houses surrounding ours and thought about how many people had seen them. I wondered how many knew that she was fucking around on me. I was past mad, I was embarrassed, I was ashamed. I wondered did people think my wife was unhappy. Did they think I couldn't satisfy her? I felt like a fool. I understand now, how Rayne must have felt every time she caught me cheating. Every time she found out that everyone knew what was going on before she did. Then it hit me, Chris was the one in the video. He was the one I saw fucking my wife. I thought of all the times he would smile and wave when we passed each other outside. I felt my blood boil.

I walked up to Chris' door and rang the bell. No one answered. I rang it repeatedly. I am not leaving without my wife. I'm standing at this man's door, ringing his bell like I'm a damn Jehovah's Witness. Finally, Chris answers the door wearing nothing but a pair of shorts. His eyes look like they are going to pop out of his head when he sees me. My intentions were to just ask for Rayne but seeing this motherfucker and knowing he had been inside my wife, pissed me off. I punched him in the face. When he fell back, I walked into the house. I pulled the pistol I was carrying out of my pocket and cracked that motherfucker over the head with it, twice. I left his punk ass on the floor whining like a little bitch. I climbed the stairs and found Rayne naked, in his bed.

She didn't look upset. She wasn't scared. I stand there, my stares are met with stares of her own. She didn't care.

"Get dressed." I ordered her. "We are going home."

"I'm not going anywhere with you and if you don't leave then I am calling the police."

"Rayne, I know you are just doing this because you are hurt but this is not you baby. You are not like this. I'm sorry. Let me make it up to you."

"I'm done with your shit, Quest. I know I've said it before but I mean it this time."

"No, you don't you are just angry. Baby, we can fix this."

I hear the sirens and so does Rayne. That scary ass bastard had called the police on me. I had been holding the gun at my side the entire time I was talking to Rayne. I point it at her.

"Get up, now." I demanded. "We are going home."

"I'm not going anywhere with you, Quest. We are done. If you want to shoot me then do it but I'm not going home with you, I'm not going to stay married to you. I'm done and nothing you do will change how I feel. I loved you more than I loved myself and you didn't care. St me, a bullet couldn't hurt any worse than the hell you've put me through at least that pain will be over quickly."

I couldn't stop the tears, I was sobbing. My heart hurt. She was willing to go through hell just to keep the relationship going and

I had taken her love for granted and now she was gone. I had thrown away a diamond to pick up rocks.

"I love you, Rayne. I always have and I always will." Was the last thing I said before I pulled the trigger.

Rayne

The police arrived shortly after Quest shot himself in the head. They called for an ambulance and I rode in it with him to the hospital, holding his hand the entire time. I told him I loved him and begged him to hold on.

We got to the hospital, where doctors and nurses dressed in sickening pea green scrubs whisked Quest away from me. I am shaken and covered in blood. I'm not crying. I'm just in shock. I pull my cell phone out and call the only two people I knew I could always count on, Corey and Zola.

"Quest shot himself in the head. We are at Grady Hospital." I say it like I am telling them about the weather. I hear my voice but it doesn't sound like me. Both say they are on their way. I hang up the phone and sit in the lobby waiting.

Zola arrives first and sits down beside me. I'm glad she doesn't ask any questions. I don't want to talk. I don't want to think. The numbness is my savior. She just puts her arms around me and we sit in silence until Corey arrives. I make the introductions when he walks into the room.

"Corey this is Zola, Zola this is Corey." I say.

"Remember we met before at your wedding Rayne." Corey reminded me.

My wedding. That's right, I remember. Corey walked me down the aisle and Zola was my maid of honor. I forgot they met at my wedding. My wedding, I started thinking about that day and how perfect it was. Quest was the love of my life. He was my entire world and I was so happy that I was going to be his wife. It was a fairytale come true. Now my life had become a nightmare.

Corey, Zola and I sat in the waiting room for hours without hearing a word on Quest's condition. Finally, a nurse came out and told us to follow her. She led us to a secluded room in the back of the emergency room. I lost it. All the emotions that I was holding in came pouring out at once. I knew what this was. They had placed my mom and I in this room when my dad had died of a heart attack. They never put you in the family room when it is good news. I am crying so hard now that I can't breathe and barely make it to the trash can before the grapefruit bitter vomit comes up.

The doctor walked in and started talking and the whole time I'm shaking my head, no. No, I don't want to hear this. No, it's been a mistake. No, stop talking, stop telling me, go back and try harder because my husband was a fighter and he wouldn't leave me. He is not gone. Stop saying that, stop talking!

"We have done all we can do. He has no brain activity. We left him on life support to give you the opportunity to say goodbye to him." The doctor stated despite my mental objections.

"I am so sorry for your loss, Mrs. Harrison. If you would like to see him then you can follow me and I will take you to him." The doctor rose from his seat and headed toward the door.

I looked at Zola and Corey and tell them I want to see Quest alone. They both nod and give me a quick hug before I leave out of the room. I walked into the room and there was Quest, lying still on crisp white sheets. I could tell his room had been cleaned, the sheets had been changed. A thick white afro of gauze covered the wound to his head. I watched the machine rise and fall at the same rate as his chest. He wasn't breathing on his own. His heart wasn't beating on its own. He was gone and all that remained was this shell of a man that I had once loved.

I bent down close to his ear. I was hoping that everything that I had been told about hearing being the last sense to go in a dying person was true.

"I love you, Quest Harrison. I hope you know that. You are my first and only true love. Rest well, baby."

Alicia

I am feeling overwhelmed. Between Giselle losing her husband and Rayne's husband committing suicide, I feel like I am in a perpetual nightmare. I just want to wake up. I tried my best to comfort Giselle but nothing I did could get through to her. After a failed suicide attempted, I convinced her to seek treatment in an in-patient psychiatric facility. She had no light in her eyes anymore. Her smile was gone. She sat in a chair and stared blankly out the window.

When I heard what happened to Quest, I tried to reach out to her but she wouldn't have anything to do with me. Baylor and I visited her and attended the funeral but she barely acknowledged me. I tried calling and she wouldn't pick up or return my calls. I didn't want anything from her, I just wanted to be there.

Every day that passed, reminded me of how special Rayne was too me. I hated how things ended between us. I wished things had been different. I got so tired of trying to get in touch with her and not getting a reply; I took a chance and just showed up at her house.

Rayne answered the door and she looked thin. She was obviously not eating. I was concerned.

"I've been trying to call you. I just wanted to check on you and make sure that you were Ok. Do you need anything?

"I'm fine." Rayne dryly replied.

"Rayne, I'm sorry."

She cut me off before I could get my apology out.

"I can either get bitter or I can get better. It's that simple. I either take what has been dealt to me and allow it to make me a better person, or I allow it to tear me down. The choice doesn't belong to fate. It belongs to me. I choose to let you go. You don't owe me an apology because there is nothing to forgive. I don't ever want to see or hear from you again."

Rayne slowly closed the door in my face. I stood on her porch, staring at her door. I was hoping that she would realize that what she was saying was a mistake. I thought she would open the door and tell me she didn't mean it; but that didn't happen. Rayne was gone forever. Why hadn't I realized before this moment that I was in love with her

Rayne – 3 months later

It's been 3 months since Quest committed suicide. I was still staying home, not taking calls, not having visitors. I just didn't want to deal with the world. Alicia/Lee reached out to me but I didn't want anything to do with her. I ended my relationship with Chris. It was just too painful of a reminder. Corey and Zola would come by and check on me. They always brought groceries, books, movies and flowers. Anything they thought would cheer me up. Nothing helped. I was depressed. I had stopped living.

I had to get out of this funk. Part of me felt guilty because I had started doing the same thing to Quest that he was doing to me. I had become a cheater and liar. I had pushed him too far. I thought that giving him a taste of his own medicine would make him finally appreciate me. If I had known, he wouldn't be able to handle it then I probably wouldn't have done the things I did.

I can't keep living like this. I called Hope's House and ask if they could come and pick up some donations. I started packing up Quest things and get them ready to be picked up. In the dresser under his t-shirt, I found the journal that Alicia had given us for our first therapy assignment.

I opened his journal and begin to read.

The things I love about Rayne:

1. She loves me despite myself
2. She loves me even when she doesn't have a reason to
3. She shows me how much she loves me everyday
4. She is the best wife ever
5. Even though she is smart, beautiful and compassionate, she still chose me

The things I would change/hate about Rayne.

1. She loves me even when I don't deserve it
2. She loves me despite how much I hurt her.
3. She is loyal even though I don't deserve her loyalty
4. She respects me even when I don't show her any respect
5. She chose me when she could have done so much better
6. I hate these things for her because they allow her to be hurt by me.

The tears were falling uncontrollably. I always thought I wasn't good enough for Quest and that is why he cheated all the time. He thought I was too good for him. He was battling demons that I knew nothing about.

I was so sick of feeling numb. I was sick of regrets and even though my heart was still broken I wanted to feel something. Anything. I got in the shower and turned the water on, making it as hot as I could stand it. The pain was excruciating but I could feel it. I felt alive for the first time in the past 3 months.

I got dressed and called Corey to tell him I was coming over.

Corey

I just got a call from Rayne. She was crying, again. I had been trying to get her out the house for the past three months and I couldn't even get her to go out to lunch. I was glad she called and was coming to visit but I had company. Sometimes females will trip over female friends. Woman can get crazy jealous even when there is nothing going on.

The doorbell rang and I unlocked the door to let Rayne in. As soon as she walked through the door she started kissing me. I'm in shock. I grabbed her shoulders and pulled her away from me. "Rayne, I know you are emotional right now, you are lonely and feeling some kind of way but this is not you."

"You don't know everything about me Corey."

"I know you are a good girl."

"Just like I said, you don't know everything about me Corey."

Rayne reached up, put her hand behind my head and pulled me down to kiss her. Honestly, over the years, I have thought about kissing her. Hell, truth be told, I had thought about doing more than kissing her. I have masturbated to fantasies of Rayne in my bed. Now here she was kissing me and it felt good. I wrapped my arms around her and pulled her tightly against me and her body feels even better than I imagined it would. Rayne put her other hand between us and began rubbing my dick through my pajama pants. My mind is screaming at me, asking me what the fuck I was doing. I have another woman in the bedroom and here I am getting it in with my BFF in the living room. While the angel and devil on my shoulders are having a heated debate about my morals, Rayne dropped to her knees and within seconds she has popped my dick out of my pajamas and has it balls deep in her mouth. My legs buckle. Fuck!!! She is sucking my dick like the cure to whatever was hurting her was in it and she was determined to get it out.

I could barely stand so I put one hand on the couch and the other on her head to steady myself. My eyes are closed; my head is back and my mouth is open. Loud moans escape my lips and I am so caught up that I have forgotten all about the woman in the next room that I had fucked earlier. I forgot about her until I heard her voice behind me.

"What the fuck, Corey!" she screamed at me.

I pulled my dick out of Rayne's mouth and turned to apologize but before I could Rayne stands up to confront the woman.

"Zola?" Rayne looked puzzled.

"Rayne?" Zola looked just as confused.

I am standing there in the middle of both with my dick still rock hard.

"I didn't know you two were dating." Rayne says still looking confused.

"We have only been dating for a short time." Zola responds almost apologetically.

"Does anybody need a drink besides me?" Corey speaks up.

"I'm sure we could all use a few right now." Zola says.

Rayne

We sit on the couch and I spill the tea to my best guy friend and my best girlfriend about how crazy my life had been even before Quest shot himself. I told them about the affair with my neighbor and sending Quest a video of it. I told them about the man I met on a website and had a one-night stand with and finally I told them about the relationship that I had been having with Alicia.

"Wait a minute." Zola speaks up. "So are you bisexual now?"

I think about it for a minute and I'm not sure how to answer that question. Lee was the only woman I had been with and I had never looked at women like that before so I don't know if I'm bisexual or if I was just attracted to Lee. I wasn't sure if I would ever be with another woman.

"I'm not sure." I finally reply. "I'm just really confused right now."

"I must admit, listening to you talk about sex with a woman has made me hot."

I go back to the time that I first met Lee and I channel her when I speak to Zola.

"Have you ever thought about kissing a girl?" I asked. "Katy Perry did and she liked it."

Zola burst into laughter. "Well, if I am going to kiss a girl it might as well be my best friend."

I leaned towards her and she leaned into me and we kiss.

"Did you like it?" I asked when she pulled away.

Instead of replying she grabbed me and started back kissing me passionately. I pulled her gown up and slide down on the floor in front of her. I put her legs on my shoulders and buried my face deep in her pussy. Zola moaned loudly. We were so caught up in the moment that I think we both forgot that Corey was even in the room until he walked over, pulled out his dick and stuck it in Zola's mouth.

"Let's move this party to the bedroom." Corey spoke up.

We break our chain and head for the bed. Zola lies down and I go back to eating her pussy. I am on my knees with my face between

Zola's legs and my ass is in the air. Corey slides in behind me and takes me doggy style and for a minute, I lose my rhythm. I was not expecting his dick to feel so good. Damn, if I had known his dick was this good, I would have given him some pussy a long time ago.

We switched positions and now Zola is lying on her back and Corey is eating her pussy while I straddled her face so she could eat mine. Zola is eating my pussy like a champion. I can't believe this is her first time. She is incredible. We put Corey on his back and Zola and I take turns giving him head, first one, then the other, then both of us together. One sucking his dick while the other sucked on his balls. We would both take our tongues and run it up and down the length of his shaft. Sometimes I would suck his dick while Zola would go up and kiss him or suck on his nipples and then we would switch. She would suck his dick while I sat on his face, grinding my pussy into his lips and tongue.

We continue our marathon love making session until 6 in the morning.

"Can we go to IHOP?" I asked.
Everyone is half asleep but also starving. We get up and get dressed and Corey drives to IHOP. Zola is in the front seat and I take the back seat. When we get to IHOP the waitress leads us to a booth and we take a seat.

"Being with both of you was the best feeling that I've ever had. I already loved you both as friends anyway and I think in a relationship you should be friends before lovers." I started explaining.

"Relationship?" Zola questioned.

"Let me finish. You two have always been there for me. You are the only two people I know that will always have my back no matter what. I look at the two of you and see that there is something already there. What I am proposing is that we commit ourselves to each other, all three of us."

"Let me get this straight. I would have two girlfriends? At the same time? Corey asked. "Sign me up.""
Zola and I both laugh simultaneously.

"I don't know." Zola says hesitantly. "How would this work? What about jealousy."

"I have never wanted anything for each of you other than for you to be happy. I know that is all that either of you have ever wanted for me. So why can't we spend the rest of our lives making each other happy?" I asked.

Both sit quietly and I can tell they are deep in thought.

I continue, "I don't want this to be a sex thing. I want us to have a real, true, and committed relationship. Corey, I am not saying this because I am lonely and missing Quest. I want to move in with you. Zola, I know your lease is up on your apartment at the end of the month. Instead of renewing it, why can't we all just live together? Corey's house is big enough for all of us. You two have always been closer to me than my biological family so why can't we become a family?"

"I'm in." Zola finally spoke up.

"Me, too." Corey agrees.

"Then by the power invested in me, I now pronounce us a triad." I say.

We all stand up and lean across the table and kiss. The look on the faces of the other people in the restaurant was priceless.

We were almost done eating when Corey said he had one question.

"You can ask me anything." I say.

"What happened to the good wholesome girl that saved her virginity for marriage?"

I thought for a minute and then responded, "Everyone changes, remember, even the devil was once an angel."

About the Author

Adisa Salim is a spoken word artist, author and motivational speaker. She was born in Illinois and raised in Alabama. Adisa is a mother, grandmother and an activist in the movement to end domestic violence.